I0603511

Dandelion Dreams

Finding Forever Book 2

USA TODAY BESTSELLING AUTHOR

AMALI ROSE

Dandelion Dreams
Copyright © 2018 by Amali Rose

This book is a work of fiction. Names and characters, places, and incidents are the product of the author's imagination or are used fictitiously. Any resemblance to actual events, locales, or persons, living or dead, is coincidental.

Editing: Stacey Broadbent & Petrina Jenkins - Spell Bound
Cover Art: Ben Ellis – Tall Story Designs
Cover Photo: Adobestock

All rights reserved. In accordance with the U.S. Copyright Act of 1976, electronic sharing of any part of this book without the permission of the publisher or author constitute unlawful piracy and theft of the author's intellectual property. If you would like to use the material from this book (other than for review purposes), prior written permission must be obtained by contacting the publisher at authoramalirose@gmail.com. Thank you for your support of the author's rights.

FBI Anti-Piracy Warning:

The unauthorized reproduction or distribution of a copyrighted work is illegal. Criminal copyright infringement, including infringement without monetary gain, is investigated by the FBI, and is punishable by up to five years in prison, and a fine of $250,000.

Dandelion Dreams

Finding Forever Book 2

USA TODAY BESTSELLING AUTHOR
AMALI ROSE

This book is for Kerry.
Because you fight. Because you are determined. Because you
have an amazing heart.
You are one of the strongest people I know.
I want to be you when I grow up.

"The world breaks everyone, and afterward, some are strong at the broken places."
Ernest Hemingway.

Synopsis

With a wild heart and a fierce spirit, Cassidy Jensen passionately lives life to the fullest, determined to embrace all it has to offer. She tells herself she's open to love, not realizing crushing guilt from a tragic loss is holding her back from ever truly getting close to someone again.

After losing her job, she's forced to take a position working alongside Mason Alexander. Without trying, he manages to be everything she doesn't want in a man: guarded, aloof, and a workaholic. The only emotion he ignites in her is absolute frustration.

From day one, there is friction between the polar opposite pair. But—as the saying goes—there is a thin line between love and hate. It doesn't take long for the sizzling chemistry between them to become temptingly palpable. With Cassidy looking at Mason in a new light, can she come to terms with the fact that what the heart wants isn't always what it needs?

ine Years Ago

My phone buzzes in my hand and I roll my eyes, laughing when I see Aidan's name on the screen. I knew he wouldn't make it through the night without calling me. Such a loser.

My loser, though.

Answering the phone with my patented Aidan greeting, "Whaddup, Boner." I hear Aidan Bonefield sigh in exasperation.

"Christ, CJ, I have to deal with that shit all the time, shouldn't my girlfriend cut me some slack?"

"Are you fucking kidding me, Boner? It's my obligation as your girlfriend to torment you with this as much as possible! Now what do you want? My girls and I are about to go get our slut on. Skye's giving me the stink eye as we speak."

I cover the receiver and glare right back at my best friend, Skye.

"Calm your juicy tits, Skyeballs, give me five minutes to deal with my Boner!" I return to my conversation with Aidan.

"CJ, what the hell do you mean 'get your slut on'?" Aidan bites out.

"Jesus, Boner, relax, it's just an expression. What do you want anyway? You're supposed to be off getting alcohol poisoning with your idiot friends."

I hear him laugh, and I swear if I had a heart, it would skip a beat. That velvety chuckle is my undoing and has me dropping my panties more often than is probably appropriate.

"Have you been up to your room since I left?"

"Nope, I got dressed in Devon's room so I could steal her clothes. Why?"

"I left something for you."

I can practically feel my eyes light up. There's nothing I like better than a surprise. Well, I mean, except orgasms, but then who doesn't love a good orgasm?

Making my way up the stairs to my room on the second floor of the dorm, I hear the muffled sounds of Aidan's loser friends in the background, and try to control my irritation. How he puts up with them I have no clue.

"Where are you guys?"

"In the car, heading to Smiley's. Jackson's our DD tonight and the asswipe won't stop bitching about it."

I snort out a laugh as I reach my door. Jackson is the

biggest douchedick around, so I find his misery highly enjoyable. Opening the door to my room I make my way inside when I hear a loud screech followed by a variety of expletives.

"Aidan? Aidan, what happened? Are you there?" I bark out the words and the anxiety in my voice is clear.

"You dickwad! Be fucking careful, asshole. Fuck! You know the roads are icy, you prick."

My heart rate returns to normal as I hear Aidan's strong voice cursing out someone, presumably Jackson.

"You okay there, Boner?"

"Yeah, we're good."

"Okay, well, tell Jackson the jackass I'm going to kick *his* ass next time I see him, for scaring me like that."

Huffing out a laugh he replies, "Yeah, I'm sure he'll be terrified, Blondie." He pauses for effect before continuing, "are you in your room yet?"

"Yep." I glance around, looking for my surprise, but seeing nothing. I'm unable to hide the disappointment in my voice. "There's nothing here! Are you screwing with me, Boner? You do remember who grants you access to the pussy parade, don't you?"

"The bed, CJ, check the bed." I can practically feel the exasperation vibrating in his voice.

Moving forward, I spot the treasure lying on my pillow.

"Aidan." My voice is barely a whisper, missing its usual bravado.

"You like it?"

I bend over and pick up the small bouquet of

dandelions he left for me. Bringing the delicate flowers to my nose, I inhale deeply, and I'm immediately overwhelmed with memories from my childhood. These flowers—my favorites—are so meaningful to me. I love that Aidan understands that this little bouquet is going to endear him to me, so much more than any big money item.

"They're beautiful, Aidan, I love…."

"FUCK!" A strangled cry from Aidan cuts me off, and my stomach plummets. The blatant terror in his voice reaches through the phone line and wraps an icy cold grip around my heart. "Aidan!" I scream as my ears are assaulted with the sound of screeching tires and splintering glass. The usual arrogant tones of boys who are still growing into men, are replaced with shrill cries of fear and panic, before an eerie silence descends, broken only by the occasional creak of mutilated metal. The dandelions drop to the floor, petals scattering.

"AIDAN!"

CHAPTER ONE

*F*ucking, *fuckity, fuckbomb.*
My hand flies up to tuck a strand of blonde hair behind my ear, but instead it begins to unconsciously twirl the silky tendril around my finger.

Breathe in. One. Two. Three. Breathe out. One. Two. Three.

"Miss. Jensen, are you listening to me?" Glancing up, I meet the watery, blue eyes of the Human Resources Manager and attempt to control the expletives that are sitting on the tip of my tongue, just waiting to burst forth.

"Yes, I am, sir." I endeavor to sound as meek as possible. No matter how much it pains me, I need to recover this situation and turn it around. I refuse to believe this cannot be fixed. "Mr. Connors, let me assure you that I could not be *more* sorry for my behavior, and I guarantee that it will never happen again." Mustering all the fake sincerity I have in me, I look across the desk and bestow a blindingly bright smile on him. Taking in the weathered, lined face of the man sitting across from me, I can't help but notice how his weary appearance is in stark contrast to the vibrancy with which I try to live my life. I do my best not to cringe as I can almost feel his apathy rub off on me.

"Miss. Jensen, you fell asleep in a meeting. A meeting where you were a representative of this firm, and in turn, presented us in a highly unprofessional manner." Sighing loudly, he rubs his eyes roughly. "Quite frankly, the crass and uncouth behavior you have demonstrated since your employment, has been appalling. You have already received three written warnings, and I'm afraid I have no choice but to let you go."

My mouth drops open in surprise. Suddenly time slows down, and my senses are heightened. I hear the ticking of Connors' wall clock, the rasp of his breath as he awaits my response. I feel the sweat break out across my brow and my heart jumps to my throat. *This can't be happening*, plays on a loop in my head. As awful as this job is, I *need* it.

"Conn- uh, I... Mr. Connors, look, I'm sure we can work something out. I agree totally that my behavior was unacceptable, and I can fully accept the need for disciplinary action, but surely dismissal is unnecessary. I mean, if I hadn't had that dream and gotten a little...um, noisy, no one would have even noticed my little nap!"

The derisive noise that escapes him, tells me that Connors isn't buying what I'm selling. Not a problem, I just need to lay it on a little thicker.

"Mr. Connors, sir, what if I agree to unpaid overtime for a month? Or, or a week of unpaid leave where I think about my behavior and—"

"This is not a negotiation, I'm sorry." Walking around his desk, he takes a seat, steepling his fingers in front of him, and meeting my eye. "Please gather your personal items from your desk, and leave the premises, Miss. Jensen. You can collect your reference letter at the front desk on your way out." Leaning back in his chair, Connors sizes me up, and for the first time since I entered his office, I sense a tiny bit of empathy. "Your administrative work here was adequate, Cassidy, and while your attitude isn't a fit for Patterson & Partners, I'm sure you will be an asset somewhere else. Perhaps in a less rigid environment. All of which has been reflected in your reference letter."

I'm still staring at him, slack jawed, as I try to make sense of what is happening. I hate this job. I've hated every office job I've ever had. But I have never once been fired from a job. People love me! I'm a fucking delight.

"That will be all, Miss. Jensen."

I realize that I am, once again, being dismissed, so I gather myself as best as I can, and begin to make my exit.

Stopping in the doorway, I slowly turn, formulating my words and deciding what I want his last impression of me to be. Classy, I decide. Classy is the smart option.

Nah, fuck that.

"Connors, dude, everyone knows that's a fucking rug on your head. And it's not even a good one. It's like an animal crawled up there, got cozy, and decided it was a good place to die. You really should do something about that, if you want people to take you seriously. Toodles!" Turning on my heel, I sashay out of the office, smirking at the sounds of indignation that follow me.

❧

Sitting on a stool, I lean back, placing my elbows on the counter behind me, and survey my surroundings. Crossing my legs, I let my heel slip and dangle from my right foot, bouncing it carelessly. Monroe's is bustling with the dinner-time rush, and while I normally enjoy people-watching, tonight the raised voices and almost frenzied atmosphere is straining my nerves.

Glancing down at my watch I see that Wyatt will be finishing up her shift in a few minutes, and Skye should be arriving any time now. My eyes scan the diner again, falling on a booth containing three teenage boys. They've been sucking down water for the past twenty minutes, and I'm ready to pounce as soon as they vacate their prime spot. The lanky, spotted one wearing a backwards baseball cap looks up and catches my eye. Leveling him with my best scowl, I throw him daggers that would put Regina George to shame. He cowers for a moment, before hastily grabbing up his things and urging his friends to do the same. In the blink of an eye, they're scampering out the door, and I throw myself into the booth.

Grabbing the menu, my eyes slide over the options

without really taking anything in. My mind is still in turmoil, trying to assess the damage from today. One thing is blindingly obvious though; I need to find a new job as soon as possible. If my dream is to ever get off the ground, I need to have an income to help finance it. And for all the boring shit too, I guess. A gal really does need food in her belly, and a roof over her head.

My mind starts to mentally scan through my professional contacts, trying to remember if I'd heard of any jobs going recently. Working in an office is as boring as fuck, so I try to keep things interesting by changing jobs often. This means I've managed to gain some inside sources over the years. However, this is the first time I have ever *needed* a new job, rather than just looking for a way to alleviate my boredom.

"Hey, Sweetie."

I startle comedically as Wyatt slides into the booth opposite me.

"Jesus fucking Christ, Red! Are you trying to kill me?"

Snickering, she rolls her eyes in response to my dramatic statement, but fuck. She just took years off my life!

"How long until Skye gets here? I'm starving."

"She shouldn't be very long. We both know what she'll get though, so we may as well put the order in." I let my eyes scan the menu one last time. Still nothing seems appetizing, so I settle on a tuna melt.

"Okay, I'll run up and give our orders to Dylan."

I watch Wyatt as she makes her way to the kitchen, all long limbs, swaying ass and graceful strides. She maneuvers through the crowd with ease, and I envy how content she seems here. Sometimes it feels like I'll never find my place in this world. Damned if I don't keep trying though.

"Ugh." Skye appears as if from nowhere and takes up a seat alongside me.

"What the fuck is up with you two scaring the shit out of me?!"

Skye fumbles with her purse, pushing me further along and getting herself situated before looking at me incredulously. "Are you serious right now? I said your name about a thousand times before I sat down, asking you to move!"

"A thousand?" I let the word fall from my mouth disbelievingly. "Well, you know, Balls, I'm glad to see you're not prone to exaggeration. I'd hate to think that Spanky wasn't really sporting an eight-inch cock."

"Cassidy! Oh my god, I have never once told you how big Ben's mmm-hmm is!"

My eyes practically pop out of my head and, as hard as I try, I can't stop the loud snort of laughter that escapes me.

Wyatt chooses this moment to return to the booth and looks between the two of us quizzically, one eyebrow raised. "Do I even want to know?"

"No." Skye's voice is firm and brokers no argument, so I roll my eyes and mouth "later" to Wyatt, which causes her to giggle. Yeah, Wyatt's a giggler. Nobody's perfect, I guess.

"Okay, why are we here, Cass?" Skye turns her

attention to me, and in a very uncommon reaction, I feel my cheeks start to pink.

"I got fired today." My words are uttered with far more confidence than I'm actually feeling, and I'm pretty damn proud that I got it out without a single waver.

Looking up, I am met with two shocked expressions, their eyes almost as wide as their mouths.

"Well, say something! Isn't this where you're supposed to offer me encouragement and tell me how everything is going to be all right?" I swing my head between my two best friends. "I've gotta say, I'm pretty disappointed in you both right now."

Skye is the first to regain control of her verbal capabilities, spewing out a bunch of platitudes while grabbing my hand in both of hers and squeezing tight. Which I'm sure is supposed to be comforting, but the reality is more excruciating than anything else.

"Cassidy, what happened?" Wyatt's voice is quietly curious, but manages to avoid any sense of attack. I think we all know that my work ethic can sometimes leave a lot to be desired, so I appreciate the restraint she's showing.

"I might have fallen asleep in a meeting." The grip on my hand loosens, and I can sense that I'm losing my audience, so I rush on. "But in my defence, I had been up the entire night before, getting an order finished. *And* nobody would have even realized I was asleep, but I started having that recurring Chris Pratt dream. You know the one where he's licking my—" Noticing the raised eyebrows and unimpressed looks I am receiving from my "friends" I decide it's best to cut that thought short. "Anyway, all I'm saying is I made a few little moans, and suddenly I'm unemployable? How is that fair?"

Skye and Wyatt look at each other across the table, and I try to gauge their reactions. I'm aware that napping during an important meeting is probably not the most professional thing I've ever done. But, Christ, being an administrative assistant, for a taxation lawyer no less, is boring as all fuck. Surely concessions need to be made to accommodate the boredom factor?

"You fell asleep *during* a meeting?" Skye's voice is brimming with barely concealed mirth. I nod my head solemnly. "So, to clarify, you fell asleep during a meeting, and then while you were asleep, you had a dirty dream about Chris Pratt—during which time, you made sex noises. And let's be clear, I was your roommate for four years, I know that your sex noises are loud and proud. That would have been quite... the aural delight for a bunch of middle-aged tax accountants, Cass." Wyatt slaps a hand over her mouth in what I assume is an attempt to hide the unattractive snort laugh that follows Skye's statement.

"Okay, it wasn't my finest moment, I am fully prepared to admit that. But I really think that thundercunt, Connors, overreacted. I mean if anything, a woman of my stature giving the old hornballs a show like that, would have *helped* them get that account."

"A woman of your *stature*?" Wyatt enquires.

"Yes, Red," I answer, trying to keep the exasperation from my voice. "I am young and hot, therefore of a high stature." I turn to Skye. "That works, yeah?" Her only response is a sigh.

"What are you going to do, Cass? Do you have any savings? You can always come and stay with Ben and I." I cringe at the thought. As much as I love my best friend, and as much as I love tormenting her boyfriend, staying with the recently reconciled couple is not in my plans.

"Thanks for the offer, Skyeballs, and as much as I would love to stay with the bonk buddies, if I was going to crash with anyone, it would be Red over here," I respond, pointing my finger at Wyatt.

Her eyes widen in surprise, with just a tiny hint of horror. To be honest, I'm slightly offended.

"Oh, yeah, of course, Sweetie. You can stay with me as long as you like."

"Relax, Wyatt." I let her off the hook. "I have the money that I was saving for a new oven. I'm good for a couple of months at least." Sighing, I finally allow the strain of today to wash over me, and my shoulders slump.

"Maybe you should take this as a sign, Cassidy." I glance up at Wyatt, as Skye sucks in a breath and starts bouncing in her seat.

"Yesssss, Cass! This is it! It's time for you to start focusing on your business! With no day job distracting you, you can start taking on more baking jobs. You've been wanting to do this for years, killing yourself to get orders done around work hours. This is perfect!" She claps her hands, practically giddy.

"Slow your roll there, Balls. That "distraction" pays

the bills, you know." My brain is scrambling, trying to come up with a valid reason why I couldn't try to kick-start my business. You know, other than because I'm scared shitless of failing. Because scared is the one thing I will never admit to being.

"It's not that easy, my schnookums. Every chick and her cute little fluffy dog has a cupcake business these days. It would take months, fuck maybe even years, to get something off the ground, let alone something successful enough that I could quit working." I lean back in the booth and take in my girls' eager faces.

"Goddammit, if I have to be the voice of reason here, we're in a fuckload of trouble, you realize that, right?"

Skye tilts her head to the side, a cute little mannerism she has when she's thinking, and carefully considers everything I have said.

"What if you could find some part-time office work, you know, a few days a week, and then you could bake the rest of the week?"

I consider this seriously. It would be great to have more time to take on extra orders. I have a small group of loyal customers who are constantly referring people to me, I just haven't had the time to say yes to them. And I would still have the safety net of a secure, paying job (as long as I could manage to stay awake from now on, that is).

"That might work," I say slowly. "It actually might be perfect." The tension starts to evaporate as I feel myself settling into this idea, and my stomach comes alive, rumbling loudly.

"Ugh, where's our food, Red? I'm starving!" My eyes scan the diner, and I release a little shriek when I see Brenda, who is working the dinner shift, headed our way with a tray full of food.

"Just a heads up, you biatches are buying me dinner tonight; we're celebrating." Holding up my water glass, I raise it high. "Cheers to Mr. Pratt and his talented dream tongue. Without whom, this opportunity never would have been thrust upon me. Much like his tongue thrust—"

"Lalalalalala." Wyatt covers her ears.

"We get the idea!" Skye shrieks.

"Jesus, when did you girls get so prudish? Fine," I raise my glass once again, "here's to part-time work. May it be easy to find, and even easier to stay awake through."

CHAPTER TWO

MASON

*F*uck. *Fucking, motherfucker.*
    I glare at the computer screen, doing everything in my power to maintain control.

Mason,

Lauren from HR has been in contact to inform me that you postponed the assistant interviews last month, and have yet to reschedule them.

Let me remind you that the temp is only contracted until the end of this week, and when I return next week I will only be working 2 days. It is urgent that you find a permanent assistant for the remaining 3 days as soon as possible.

Regards,
   Tanya.

P.S. Get your shit together, Mason. I have a baby now, I can't be working around the clock for you. You better have hired someone by the time I'm back or I'm going to kick your ass. Sir.

Reaching over, I press the button on the intercom and wait for the static to subside before barking out, "Denielle, get in here. Now!"

Ten seconds later, my temp, or as I like to call her, the pain in my ass, ambles into my office, already playing nervously with her auburn hair. She looks lost and a tiny bit terrified. Good.

"You rescheduled those assistant interviews like I asked, didn't you?"

Her eyes widen, and I can practically see her mind working overtime in an effort to find a plausible excuse for her incompetence. Incompetence that I have been suffering through for the last four months.

"Sir, I am so sorry. I meant to do it a couple of weeks ago. In fact, I wrote it on a Post-it note and stuck it to my computer, but it must have gotten thrown out when I cleaned my desk. At your insistence." My mind wanders briefly to that day, when after waiting twenty-five minutes for her to find one file, I demanded she clean the sty she called a desk. However, my thoughts are cut off when Denielle continues, "You really should have reminded me, sir."

I feel my temper flame, the back of my neck burning as I let those words sink in.

"Denielle, you are my assistant. I give you tasks to complete, and it is your job to do them. You are not a child, and you damn well shouldn't need me riding you constantly to do your job properly." I am doing my best to reign in my annoyance, but as I stare at the woman in front of me, who is staring back somewhat defiantly, I am struggling. "Get on the phone to HR right now, and get as many of those interviews rescheduled for tomorrow as you can."

Turning to leave, Denielle bolts for the door, eager to make her escape.

"Denielle?" She stops abruptly and turns to face me, almost reluctantly. "You can be assured that my dissatisfaction with your performance these last few months will be noted in my report to your agency." Her face starts to crumple, but I turn away and redirect my attention toward my computer screen before I can see any tears.

"The interviews, Denielle. Now, please."

Three hours later, I'm fucking livid as I am informed that none of the prospective assistants are still available, and while HR are scrambling to find new candidates, it's unlikely to happen before the end of the week.

Rubbing my forehead, where I can feel the onset of the mother of all headaches, I grimace as I imagine all the ways Tanya is going to make me suffer for this monumental screw up.

My cell begins vibrating on the desk, and the sound of the phone scratching along the surface irritates my already frayed nerves. Snatching it up, I answer unthinkingly, my mind still stuck on the assistant problem.

"What?"

"Jesus, man, what crawled up your ass?" I sigh as the voice of my best friend, Ben, snaps back at me.

"An incompetent idiot masquerading as an assistant, that's what. What do you want, Mackinnon?"

"I'm just reminding you that you agreed to play basketball with the guys tonight. I'm the lucky bastard that got tasked with getting your ass down there. So be there, asshole."

"Ah, fuck." Scrubbing a hand over my face, I mentally scan my afternoon schedule. "I'm not sure I can. I have a conference call at four, which could last either five minutes or five hours, depending on how assholery my client is feeling today. Then I'm probably going to have to redraft a contract..." My voice trails off as my eyes jump around the office. As if somehow I'll find the answer amongst the modern, streamlined furniture that I hate. I could delegate the conference call to Samuels, my second in command. He has been asking for more responsibility, but I'm the first to admit that I suck at giving up control. "No, okay, I'll be there."

"Yeah?" Ben sounds doubtful, and I can't say I blame him.

"Count me in. Six, like usual?"

"Yeah. Got time for a beer after?"

My first instinct is to refuse, but after the day I've had, the idea of returning to the office with takeout that will end up cold and uneaten, holds little appeal.

"Yeah, that'd be good. See you then." Hanging up, I lean back in my chair and close my eyes, giving myself a moment as the stress of the day gets to be too much. The past year, since being appointed to CEO of Cook Enterprises, has been everything I thought it would be. Hard work, long days and every moment of elation has been countered by ten moments of frustration. But I knew it would be like this going into the role; it's what I expected. And yet I don't feel the sense of satisfaction I had anticipated. I'm right where I've always wanted to be. Where I've worked so hard to be. But it never seems to get easier. The work hours don't get any shorter, and the huge title that has been bestowed upon me seems to weigh me down, rather than give me the freedom I had always expected. In short, I'm beginning to question if everything I fought for, and sacrificed, has been worth it.

I almost groan out loud as the whiskey is slid in front of me, my lips twitching in anticipation. Out the corner of my eye I see Ben watching me with a quirked eyebrow. Choosing to ignore him, I raise the glass to my lips, and take my first sip of the amber liquid, letting the burn calm my mind.

"How have you been, man? I feel like I haven't seen you in months. You still dating that girl, Stella?"

"I don't know if you could call it dating, she's as busy as I am. We hook up every so often." I can see the cogs turning in Ben's head, and I know what's coming. Since he met his girlfriend, Skye, he's been a lovesick idiot, and he's lucky I'm as busy as I am, or he would be getting a lot more shit about it. But my arrangement with Stella works. She is one of the top lawyers in New York, at the top of her game. She's smart, elegant and all class. The epitome of everything I should be looking for in a woman. The reality however, is that neither of us have time to dedicate to a relationship, so we settle for a casual fuck whenever the tension gets too much. Speaking of which, it's probably time I gave her a call.

"You know, Mase, maybe it's time to start looking for something serious? You're almost thirty years old, man, aren't you tired of fucking around? What about your new assistant, is she hot? You spend most of your life at that place, maybe a little office romance could lead to something more?"

"You do realize you're sounding like my mother, right?" My lips tilt up in a small smirk before the mention of my assistant brings my mood crashing back down. "Besides, don't even get me started on the shit show that hiring a new assistant has turned into. Somehow, the temp screwed up and now I am assistant-less on the days Tanya isn't working. She's going to cut my balls off with a blunt and rusty knife when she finds out."

Ben cringes, his hand subconsciously goes straight to his dick, which provides me with my first laugh of the day.

After ordering another whiskey, I turn back to Ben and am faced with an expression I haven't seen in a long time. In fact, the last time I saw that face was when he decided it would be a great idea to streak across our college campus, naked. In the middle of January. It's a good bet that whatever he's about to propose will end just as badly.

"Cassidy got fired yesterday."

I try to follow his train of thought. I've only had one drink so it shouldn't be too hard, but fucked if I know what he's talking about.

"Okay? Sucks to be Cassidy, I guess." Ben nods his head, as though this conversation didn't just take a weird-as-fuck turn. "Who the hell is Cassidy, BJ?"

Ben glares at me, his eyes squinting in that way they do anytime I use his initials.

"She's Skye's best friend, loser, and if you ever tell her that my initials are BJ, I will fucking take you down."

"Best friend? You mean the crazy one?" I vaguely remember Ben telling me she had a mouth on her that would rival Kanye.

"I mean, she's not actually crazy." His brow furrows.

"At least I'm pretty sure she's not. She did threaten to cut off my dick once, though, so I guess it's a coin toss." Again, his hand finds his junk as though checking to make sure it's still there. "Anyway, she works as an admin assistant, and has heaps of experience. She could probably help you out. Even if it's only temporarily. It might keep your balls safe from Tanya, anyway." Pausing, he lifts his beer to his mouth and takes a long pull before regarding me with a look of confusion. "Why the fuck are the women in our lives so determined to cut our junk off?"

I huff out a laugh, before considering what he's said. "Why did she get fired?"

Ben's eyes immediately leave mine and fall to the floor. A sure sign that he's about to lie his ass off.

"Uh, I'm not really sure… but I'm positive it wasn't anything serious. Nothing like falling asleep in a meeting." His right hand nervously grasps his neck and begins rubbing.

"Wait, that was really random, why would you—"

"Mase," he cuts me off, before I can finish forming my thought. "Do you really have any other option? She's the answer to your prayers, even if it's only for a couple of weeks. What do you have to lose?"

I sigh in resignation as I contemplate what he has said. Eyeing off the golden liquid in the tumbler I'm holding, I toss it back and slam the glass down on the bar.

"Can she start on Monday?"

CHAPTER THREE

CASSIDY

*M*y heels click loudly on the marble floor as I hastily make my way through the cavernous lobby of the Cook Enterprises' office building. This morning could not have been more of a shit show. After staying up until two o'clock this morning, trying to perfect a new banoffee cupcake recipe, I slept through my alarm. Or I forgot to set it. Either way, the result was me having to haul ass today, my *first* day in a new job. Add to that no hot water, and then not being able to find a clean bra, I was ready to fuck today right off.

I impatiently tap my fingernails on my purse as I wait for the elevator to arrive, and as I step inside I attempt to compose myself in the thirty seconds or so I have before I have to face the dreaded Mason Alexander.

Skye has been preparing me all weekend for the job. Apparently, this guy is a complete workaholic who buries himself in paperwork with no time for anything, or anyone, else. So, you know, your average white-collar asshole. I roll my eyes at the memory of Skye's denial. *"No, Cass, he's really very sweet. He's just... focused, that's all."* Whatever. I've dealt with the worst, and one cunt cracker is the same as the next.

As the elevator dings its arrival at the seventy-fourth floor, I quickly smooth down my newly pinked hair. It was a moment of madness the day after my dismissal, and I had assumed I would have time to change it back to my natural blonde before I started interviewing. This job fell in my lap though, and I figure that technically I am the one doing the favor here, so Mr. Alexander will just have to deal.

I step out of the elevator into the most luxurious office space I have ever seen. My heels immediately sink into the plush carpet, and I am already itching to yank these torture devices off my feet and feel the lushness beneath them barefoot. However, a quick glance around at all the buttoned-up suits bustling through the space, tells me that wouldn't be the smartest thing to do.

I head over to what appears to be the receptionist for the floor, and introduce myself.

"Miss. Jensen, I'm Kimberly, it's lovely to meet you. I'm afraid you are quite late, and Mr. Alexander is a little... um... irate?" Kimberly's kind face is creased in concern, and I find myself anxious to soothe her concerns.

"Oh, yeah, this morning has been a royal fuck up since the minute I opened my eyes, Kim, can I call you

Kim? Just point me toward Mr. Alexander's office and I will have him sorted in no time." I throw her a wink for good measure. Never let them see you sweat, right? Fake it 'til you make it, and all that shit.

Kimberly's eyes widen in surprise before a small smile appears.

"Straight down that hall," she points to her right, "it's the suite of offices at the very end. I'm sure you'll hear him." She smiles broadly at that. "I would wish you good luck, but somehow I think Mr. Alexander is the one that needs it."

Smirking, I thank her and head to face the music.

As I approach the office, I realize that Kim wasn't joking. I hear a strong, distinctly masculine voice, that I have no doubt could talk the panties off any girl under normal circumstances. Unfortunately for me, on this occasion the voice also sounds distinctly pissed off.

Following the sound of the gruff intonations, I find myself standing in the doorway to an office that is roughly the same size as my apartment. Leaning against the doorframe, I fold my arms across my chest and feel my eyes narrow as I take in the man in front of me. He's hot. The so-hot-I-would-strip-naked-and-blow-him-if-he-even-looked-in-my-direction type of hot. His light brown hair is a tousled mess. Judging by his demeanour this is most likely the result of him running his hands through it in exasperation, however, it looks more like the hair of someone freshly fucked. His skin is sun kissed to perfection, and there is a light scruff covering his jaw that I instinctively want to lick. But more than his physical appearance, it's the way he holds himself. He grips the phone receiver in his right hand, and talks in a calm voice that belies the antagonism his features portray. As he listens to the voice on the other end, his eyes glaze over with a hint of malice, while a slight sneer lifts his lip. I'm not going to lie, it's kind of a turn on. I find myself subconsciously licking along my bottom lip before realising and putting it on lock down. A man in a suit is not for me, no matter how fuckable, or lickable, he may be.

I notice Mason see me out the corner of his eye, and I try to school my features into an acceptable look of deference. I've learned over the years that it helps if the employer at least feels like they're the one in charge. Even if that is usually far from the truth.

He swivels his chair around, so he is facing me as he brusquely ends his conversation. As his heated gaze meets mine, I clench my thighs together and do my best to contain the shiver that travels down my spine.

"You're late." His tone is harsh, and the hostility in his voice gives me a moment of pause. I promised Skye I would be nice to the assmunch, but seriously, if he wants to play it this way, then my inner bitch is ready to throw down.

"Well, aren't you just a little ray of sunshine," I state, sardonically.

"I expect my assistant here at eight o'clock sharp, Miss. Jensen. Not," he raises the cuff of his shirt to check the time on what I imagine is a six-billion-dollar Rolex, "eight fifty-seven."

I mentally assess the situation. I honestly hadn't planned on getting off to such a rocky start, so I figure it's time to play the friend card. Let's give Mr. Alexander a gentle reminder that I am indeed doing him a favor.

"So, you're Spanky's best friend, huh?" My stare is assessing. "Hmm… I don't see it."

Mason's eyes spark with something indecipherable. Something that I find myself desperately wanting to figure out.

"And why is that?"

"I mean, Ben is so goofy, and you…" I trail off as I try to decide how best to phrase the next part. How do I politely say you have a stick up your ass? "You seem to be more of a stick-up-your-ass type of guy." Yep, nailed it.

His eyes dance with amusement, but only for a brief moment, before the shutters come down.

"Your desk is out there." Mason points to a desk in the outer office that faces his door. "You should find everything you need. I'm in meetings all day today, and am not to be disturbed under any circumstances. My real assistant's phone number is on the desk. She has asked that you call her first thing, so she can run you through some things. One of which will be how to best deal with me, I'm sure." I nod as I take in everything he's throwing at me.

"Put me through to Samuels on extension three, and then get me a coffee. Black, one sugar. Kimberly can show you where the kitchen area is. Actually, she can show you where everything is. I don't have time today. Thank you, Miss. Jensen." And just like that I am dismissed.

Making my way to my new desk, I am already plotting the many ways I can make Sunshine's life miserable. Although, I really do need this pay check, so I may have to settle for slightly uncomfortable. Oh well, I can have fun with that too.

"Skyeballs, you need to relax, everything is going fine." I huff out a sigh of exasperation.

"Are you sure? Because the way I hear it, Mason has developed a serious aversion to coffee." Skye quirks an eyebrow, and her voice is full of condemnation, so I do my best to suppress a smile.

"Look, I'm new. I'm still learning where everything is, that was a complete accident." My eyes widen in an effort to convey innocence.

"You put salt in his coffee, instead of sugar. Twice."

"Ugh, Balls, they were *right next* to each other. That's just asking for trouble."

"Get help, Cass." She raises a hand to silence my protestations. "Get. Help."

I snort out a laugh as I raise my glass to my lips, grateful that Skye clearly hasn't heard about any of my other "accidents". Three weeks in, and tormenting Mason has become a definite perk of this job.

Turning slightly, I let my eyes wander over the crowd in Maybe Mae's. It's surprisingly busy for a Wednesday night and, as always, the clientele is a varied mix of characters, which is one of the things I love most about this cocktail bar. Stopping short, my eye twitches involuntarily as I notice a tall, bearded man leaning against the back wall, engrossed in conversation with an equally hipster-looking guy. *Shit.* I swing myself back around on the stool to face the bar, and find Skye sipping on her second Pina colada, deep in discussion with the bartender, Ashley.

Pulling on her sleeve, I throw Ashley an apologetic look before interrupting. "We need to go. Now." I'm up and on my feet, grabbing my purse and putting on my coat, all before Skye has even placed her glass back on the bar.

"What? Why?"

"I'll explain in a minute, just move!" I hastily grab her things and throw them at her as I take hold of her elbow and drag her out of the bar.

We practically fall out into the street, and Skye immediately turns on me. "What the hell was that all about, Cass?"

Taking hold of her hand, I pull, and we fall in with the crowd, moving forward and away from what would have been an ugly confrontation.

"Dash was there."

"Dash, your boyfriend, Dash?" Skye's confusion is evident.

"He was never my boyfriend, babes, you know that."

"Were you dating him regularly?"

"Yes."

"Were you sleeping with him?"

"Well, I was fucking him, not a lot of sleeping was had." I roll my eyes.

"Were you doing both of these things exclusively, for more than three months?"

I sigh in resignation. "You know we were."

"Then he was your boyfriend, Cass, whether you want to admit it or not."

"Jesus, fine, but you can now consider him my *ex*-boyfriend, okay?"

Skye links her arm with mine, and leans her head on my shoulder. It's comforting, I admit, but it also makes walking fucking difficult.

"What happened?" Her voice is soft, and holds that imploring tone that always seems to get me spilling my guts.

"It didn't feel right, so I ended it. End of story."

"Okay." She lifts her head and stares at me, but I refuse to make eye contact, instead keeping mine fixed straight in front of me. "What didn't feel right?"

"Drop it, Balls, okay. I don't want to talk about it." I feel her instinctively tense up, and she pulls away from me.

"Would you drop it if the roles were reversed, Cassidy? No, you would be on my ass until I gave you every last detail. So, spill."

I hate that she's right. I would never let her get away with shit like this. We tell each other everything. But I'm so tired of the whole game lately. Meet someone who seems like a good guy. Have fun. Get attached. Then discover said guy is nothing like he presented to you. They lie. They use. They manipulate. And then when they're done, they make you the villain so they can walk away with a clear conscience. I've grown weary of it all, and it's so much easier to cut and run before I get hurt.

"He just isn't right for me. I don't know why, he just isn't…"

"Aidan?" Shock causes my eyes to snap to hers, and I feel like she's punched me in the gut. No one has said his name to me in a long time. We tiptoe around the subject, talking in metaphors, dancing around it in an effort to allow me to maintain the facade of someone who has moved on. But I haven't, and Skye is absolutely right. I had the perfect guy. My first love was perfect, and I have no idea how I'm supposed to replace that with something that doesn't ignite my heart, the way he did. I'm not even sure I want to try anymore.

"Balls, please," I beseech her.

"Okay, I'll drop it. Just let me say one thing. Please."

"Can I stop you?"

"Nope." She pulls me back into her, offering me support, both physically, and emotionally.

"Aidan was a wonderful boy, and he loved you intensely. But you were both nineteen, you were so young, and everything is intense and passionate when you're nineteen. I know that you loved each other fiercely, and what happened destroyed you. But do you ever wonder if you're idealizing him?" I feel the denial bubbling up in my throat, but Skye continues before I can verbalize it. "You two had only been together for four months, Cass. You hadn't really experienced anything as a couple yet. You hadn't ever had to fight for each other, or with each other. I'm worried you're rejecting amazing guys because they can't live up to the memory of a ghost."

As the words leave Skye's mouth, I can't help thinking of Mason, which has been happening more than I care to admit lately. He's the polar opposite of Aidan, and yet I can't ignore the way he excites my mind. He's everything I never wanted in a man. Plus, if I'm being honest, my pussy is kind of a fan too.

"I hear what you're saying, Skyeballs, and I promise to consider it. Can we change the subject now, please?"

"Ugh, fine!" She takes hold of my hand and we walk in silence for a few minutes. "Oh, wait. Why did we have to run from Dash? I mean I get that it would have been uncomfortable, but your race to get us out of there was a bit excessive."

"Um, he didn't really care for the way I broke up with him." My voice carries a meekness that it so very rarely holds.

"Cassidy Jensen, what did you do?"

I consider how I'm going to answer this. She's definitely not going to like the answer, and in hindsight it probably wasn't my finest moment, no matter how good my intentions were. "I broke up with him with a fruit basket."

"You what?!" Her voice has that annoying screechy quality it gets when she's appalled by my behaviour.

"What? He likes fruit! I thought it would kind of help let him down gently."

"And?"

"It did not. I have many angry voicemails that can attest to that."

"Oh my god, Cass, what am I going to do with you?" She throws her hands up, and I can't help but laugh at her indignation.

"Tolerate me, Balls. You're going to keep tolerating me." I plant a giant kiss on her cheek, before pulling away. "Now, let's get you home to Spanky."

CHAPTER FOUR

MASON

I lift my coffee cup to my nose and take a sniff. *What the fuck are you doing, Alexander?* It's not like I could smell the salt, even if she had added it again. Sighing, I decide not to risk it. As I place the mug on my desk, the intercom buzzes, startling me. Mocha liquid spills over my desk. "Fuck!"

Turning to my left, I see Cassidy smirking at me through the open door. "What!" I thunder. Shaking her head, she points to the phone. Fuming, I reach over to press the intercom button. "This better be good."

"There's a Rhonda Carter on the phone for you, Mr. Alexander." Her voice is all sweetness and light. A stark contrast to the devil horns that must be hidden under those cotton-candy locks.

"Thank you. Grab some paper towels, and get in here to clean this mess up."

The phone buzzes again. "What?" I bite out in exasperation.

"What's the magic word, Sunshine?" comes the lilting reply.

I squeeze my eyes shut, and count to ten. "Please."

"Be right there."

Sighing, I grab the phone receiver and bring it to my ear. "Hi, Mom. What's up?"

"Hi, honey. I'm just calling to make sure you'll be at dinner tomorrow night. I didn't want you to forget."

"I haven't forgotten, Mom, it's on my calendar, I'll be there."

There's a pause before my mother's voice finds my ear. "You sound stressed, Mason. Are you okay?"

Pinching the bridge of my nose in an attempt to stem the headache I feel approaching, I consider her question.

"Yeah, I'm fine. Just tired. We're close to finalizing the Thompson account, so there's been a lot of late nights. Plus, Tanya's baby has been unwell, so my second assistant has had to step up and work more days. Which in itself has been stressful. There's a bit of tension there, I'm afraid."

"With Cassidy?" My mother can't disguise the surprise in her voice, although I doubt she tried to.

"Miss. Jensen. Yes."

"Oh my goodness, Mason. That girl is delightful. We just had a long chat before she put me through to you."

Looking up, I watch as Cassidy enters my office and walks over to my desk. She moves slowly, deliberately. Her hips swaying in a way that I have no business noticing. Reaching me, she pulls my chair out, and rolls me away, before leaning over and wiping up the coffee remnants. Her ass swings in front of me, in a way I find wholly captivating, and I feel my eyes following each movement; wondering what that ass would look like as I slapped it while slamming into her from behind. Would she scream out, or would she bite down on a pillow and moan silently? Feeling my dick start to stir, I shake my head and attempt to drag myself out of the gutter my mind seems intent on crawling into.

"Is that so? A long chat?" With her back to me, Cassidy stills at the sound of my words. Straightening, she turns around and bestows a smile upon me that could light up Times Square, before throwing me a wink and making her way out of my office.

"She really is very sweet, Mason, you need to not be so tough on people. The job isn't the be all and end all for everyone the way it is for you. Some people like to enjoy their work, you know."

I ignore the wry tone in her voice as I automatically jump to defend myself. "I enjoy my work, Mom."

"Do you?" Her voice is soft, and somewhat hesitant. "You haven't seemed happy for a while now, Mase. Since the promotion, really. You know it's okay to admit you're not fulfilled. It's never too late to make a change. You're still so young, and you've set yourself up financially. Don't stagnate in a melancholy life, just because you're afraid to admit you made a mistake, my sweet boy."

I feel my stomach drop as my mother puts into

words everything I've been feeling. The consuming fear that I've wasted my life chasing something that will never satisfy me. And how incredibly pissed off that makes me.

"Well, that got very deep, very quickly! Don't mind me, sweetheart. I just worry that's all." I hear her try to inject enthusiasm into her words and notice how strained she sounds.

"You sound tired, Mom. What's been going on?"

"Oh, just these night shifts. I'm getting too old for them," she replies with a soft chuckle. With those words I'm reminded exactly why I have busted my ass since I was ten years old, to end up right where I am. The hours of study to earn the scholarships. The hours of overtime to prove myself.

"I thought you were going to scale back your shifts, not pick up nights. If you need money just tell me."

"It's not your job to take care of me, Mason." My mother's voice is stern, and I can imagine the vexed look she is wearing right now.

"Mom, you've taken care of me my entire life. Now I'm in a position where I can help you. Let me." The light on my phone for extension three begins flashing, reminding me of all the work I have to do before I can leave the office tonight. "I'm sorry, I have to go, but I'll see you tomorrow night, okay?"

"Okay, sweetheart. I love you."

"Love you too." Leaning over to answer my other line, I make a mental note to transfer some cash into my mother's account tonight.

"Yes?"

"Mason, we have a problem, man. Thompson has found an issue with clause eighty-seven ten in the contract, and is threatening to pull out of negotiations."

"Shit. Okay, get Stacey, Rob, Joel, Anthony and Joanne assembled in conference room one right now. Let them know it's going to be a late one and apologize."

"On it." Samuels hangs up and I take a deep breath while I try to formulate a game plan. Suddenly feeling constricted, I loosen my tie and undo the top two buttons of my shirt. Fuck, I can't breathe. Pushing away from my desk, I grab my cell phone and pocket it before walking out of my office, mentally making a list of the documents I need Cassidy to gather. Spotting her in front of the window, talking on her phone in a hushed tone, I stalk over, ready to ream her out. Noticing her hunched shoulders and the tension in her jaw, I pull up short and unabashedly eavesdrop on her conversation.

"Bubs, calm down, it's going to be okay, I promise." Her voice is gentle, and full of compassion for whoever is on the other end of the line. This is a side to her I haven't seen before; I'm more familiar with the antagonistic persona that I seem to bring out in her.

"Lay, breathe, baby. Is Evie there with you? Okay good, just hold tight, bubs, I'll be there as soon as work is finished. Please don't cry." Her body slumps as if overcome with fatigue, and I watch in wonder as this person who has become an intrinsic part of my life over this past month, morphs into someone completely unrecognizable.[PJ2] My chest tightens as this bold, passionate, slightly crazy woman is brought to her knees in empathy for someone she obviously cares for. My conscience gets the best of me, and I move away to give her some privacy, but in doing so, I inadvertently bump into her desk, causing a little cupcake figurine to topple over.

Cassidy swings around, and her blue eyes widen in surprise. She briskly ends the call before throwing an apologetic look my way.

"I'm sorry about that."

"It's fine. Is everything okay?" Cassidy eyes me dubiously, and I can't say I blame her.

"My baby sister. She's having some boy trouble." She shrugs her shoulders, and my eyes are drawn to the graceful slope of her neck. I notice some tattooed script along her right collarbone. The tail end is just peeking out under her white sweater, and I find my fingers twitching, wanting to explore and discover the words she found so meaningful that she tattooed them on her body.

"You can take off for the day, I'll be fine here. You go." The words have left my mouth before I even realize what I'm saying, and even after I realize the idiocy of what I've just done, I have no desire to change my mind.

"Seriously?" Even as she questions me, Cassidy is putting her jacket on and gathering her purse. "Are you sure?" This is thrown over her shoulder as she makes her way down the hall. Stifling a smile, I wave her off and watch her race away. She flies around the corner, headed for the elevator when a wave of dread washes over me. This woman is going to be trouble. She is a mess of contradictions, both enchanting and bewildering. If I'm not careful, she'll be my undoing.

CHAPTER FIVE

CASSIDY

Staring out my window, I zone out as my arm starts to ache from mixing the batter as quickly as I possibly can. Forcing myself to push through, I focus on a single bird swooping through the sky. *Yep, I can do motherfucking zen just as good as anyone*, I think smugly. Although come to think of it, can it be considered achieving zen if you're *thinking* about achieving it? I mean does my mind need to be completely emp— *ding.* The timer alerts me that I have been beating the batter long enough. *Thank Christ.* Pouring the cake mixture carefully into the lined cases, I mentally scan through everything I need to continue. This weekend has been crazy as I busted my ass to complete this order. Two dozen cupcakes, a mixture of banana caramel, chocolate indulgence, strawberry shortcake and my very own chocolate, peanut butter and M&M recipe. I can't contain my pride as I peruse the already completed treats, all boxed up and ready to go. Marking things off my checklist, I realize I am practically done. The last six cupcakes are now in the oven, and the cream cheese frosting is all prepared and ready to be applied as soon as the cakes have cooled down. I glance down at the flashing clock on the microwave, and see that I still have four hours before Tamara, one of my best customers, will be here to collect her order which is destined for her daughter, Katrina's, baby shower this afternoon.

I have to admit, designing these cakes was an experience. I deeply regret Googling 'baby shower cakes'. Bodily fluids have no place in cake decoration.

Grabbing a water out of the fridge, I flop down on the sofa and immediately get lost in the giant cushions. The vibrant yellow usually perks me up, but right now I am so exhausted I don't think anything could do it.

While trying to decide if I can be bothered moving to the bathroom to indulge in a bubble bath while I wait, my phone vibrates on the coffee table. Looking over, my heart stutters in a completely juvenile manner when I spot *Sunshine* flashing on the screen. I quickly school my features into a scowl. I find it helps keep my inner hornball on lockdown.

Snatching up the phone, I swipe the screen and bark out my greeting. "It's 10 am on a Sunday, what the fuck do you want, Sunshine?"

"Always a delight, Crazy, not much of a morning person, huh?"

"What. Do. You. Want? Wait, did you just call me crazy?" My voice rises to a level that I'm pretty sure only dogs can hear, as I practically growl with indignation. His answering chuckle does little to calm me.

"Look, as you pointed out, it is the weekend, so technically, we're off the clock, and I'm not your boss. And you have to admit, you are a *little* bit crazy."

"Well," I sulk. "It's still not polite to point it out."

"Noted. Look, I'm afraid I need a favor. I hate to ask, and trust me, I really do hate to ask, but I seem to have misplaced my key to the filing cabinets in my office, and I need it quite urgently. I don't suppose you could bring your key in?" I let his request sink in momentarily, while I try to figure out if I'm pissed at, or impressed by, his audacity.

"Let me get this straight. You want me to come in to the office now. *On a Sunday.* You want me to spend forty-five minutes on the subway, just so I can walk in, hand you a key, and then turn around and spend another forty-five minutes on the subway to get home. Is that what you're asking me?"

"Yes." At least he has the good sense to sound contrite, but that doesn't stop the snort of condescension that escapes me. "Wait, no, take a cab, and I'll pay for it. Both ways." Much better. He's a quick study, I can work with that. I pause for effect. I know I can make it back in plenty of time to finish the last cupcakes before Tamara arrives at three o'clock. Still. He deserves to sweat for a minute.

"Ugh, fine."

"And you'll come straight away? I really do need a file from there as soon as possible."

Looking at the clock, I see the cupcakes have another thirty minutes left in the oven.

"Yep, I'm leaving right now." Hanging up the phone,

I lay back down on the sofa with a satisfied smile lighting my face.

🐌

An hour later I stroll into Mason's office, and one look at his murderous expression makes traipsing down here on my day off totally worth it. Sitting behind his desk, he has both his laptop and his computer open, each screen displaying a number of spreadsheets. I can't help thinking what a depressing way to spend your weekend that must be.

"Aw, why so blue, Sunshine?"

"You said you were coming straight down here, it's been an hour. I've been sitting here twiddling my fucking thumbs for an hour." The ferocity of his tone matches his expression, and I just about squeal with glee.

"Yeah, sorry about that. I had cupcakes in the oven." Shrugging, I hand over the key he has been so desperate for, and turn to leave.

"Cupcakes? You... bake?" He sounds so confused, and for some reason I find myself feeling defensive.

"Yes, I bake. Why is that so strange?"

I've never seen him so lost for words, and if I didn't have the feeling that I was being insulted right now, I would be thoroughly enjoying his discomfort. But I do, so I'm not.

"You just don't seem like the baking type, I guess."

"The baking *type*?" I practically spit the last word out. "What the hell does that even mean?"

He at least has the good grace to look embarrassed as he considers his response.

Gripping the back of his neck, and rubbing it with a pained look on his face, I am momentarily distracted as I watch his large hand knead the skin beneath it. Yeah, hand porn. It's real, and it's beautiful.

"Look, I guess I just think of women who bake as kind of sunshine and rainbow types. And you're more... a fire and brimstone kind of gal."

My feet move toward him completely of their own volition while I quietly seethe. "I. Am. Not. I am a sweetheart. I love unicorns and shit."

"Oh well, if you love unicorns, that changes everything," he scoffs.

I glare up at him, my neck craning as his six-foot-three frame towers over me. He glowers right back at me, and as his chest rises, it brushes against my breasts, and I realize how close we are standing. The atmosphere changes in that one moment, the air now thick with tension. I desperately want to touch him, to run my palm along the scruff that constantly covers his jaw. Maybe stand on my tip toes and brush my lips across his. I squash the impulse though, knowing it won't be enough. Knowing that the desire to follow through and fuck the deliciousness standing in front of me will be too much to resist. I'm a woman who tends to act recklessly when emotions and sex are involved, but the need to protect this, whatever *this* is, overwhelms me; even in the face of my impulsive nature.

I move to take a step back but stop when Mason raises his hand and cups my face. His thumb gently

49

swipes along my cheek before he removes it and I see a small smudge of frosting on the tip. Raising his thumb to his mouth, his tongue sneaks out and licks it clean. My pussy throbs at the sight before Mason's following smirk brings me back to my senses.

"Shit." My hand flies to my face, scrubbing, in an effort to remove any other stray traces of icing. The mood broken, Mason backs away, his grin growing at my struggle, before he shrugs. "So, you bake. It's nice to have a hobby, I guess."

My eyes narrow, and once again I am reminded that this guy is a grade-A asshole. No matter how intensely my body reacts to him, or how many moments we have, I can't go there. It would only end in murder. His, obviously, and orange really isn't my colour.

"You really are an assmunch, aren't you? It's not a hobby, it's a business. A rapidly growing business. So shove that up your ass and rotate on it." I turn on my heel and start to storm out when his deep voice stops me in my tracks.

"Cassidy, wait." I pause on the threshold to his office, in two minds whether to continue or not.

"I'm sorry. I didn't mean to be an asshole, you just surprised me, that's all." I look back over my shoulder, and seeing that he looks suitably repentant, I turn and lean against the doorframe, arms crossed over my chest. Watching him take a seat at his desk, I'm reminded of my first day, and my first sighting of him. He's still blowably hot, I can't deny that. It's just a pity his personality is more prick than prince.

"What's your business name?"

"Huh?" His question rouses me from my thoughts.

"What do you call this 'rapidly growing business'?"

Ignoring his tone that is straddling the line of snide and condescension, I answer shortly. "Cupcakes by Cassidy." He lifts an eyebrow, and I have this odd feeling that I've disappointed him.

"Not particularly original, is it?"

My jaw clenches at his remark. Is he purposely trying to piss me off? Because if he is, he's doing a fucking spectacular job.

"It's not so easy to come up with a name, you know," my voice sounds petulant, even to my own ears. "Cupcakes by Cassidy is easy to remember. It does the job."

"I guess. I just never figured you for someone who would settle for mediocre. But it's really none of my business." I feel my shackles rise even further, and I'm about to launch into a counter attack when he continues. "Bring some cupcakes in this week, and we'll use them in meetings. If they're good, we may be able to look at contracting you for some freelance catering. No guarantees, obviously."

My mouth drops in surprise, and he laughs at my reaction. "Close your mouth, Crazy, you'll catch flies. I can be a nice guy. Now get out of here, I have work to do, and you're a distraction." He throws me a wink before returning to his work, and I make my way out of the office wondering what the hell just happened.

CHAPTER SIX

MASON

I throw my pen down on the desk and a low, pained groan escapes me. This account is doing my fucking head in. Although, if I'm being honest with myself, they all do. Dealing with arrogant, entitled assholes day in and day out. Kissing those asses just so I can get a signature on a dotted line. That will then increase the bottom line for another bunch of selfish asswipes. Asswipes who happen to own this company. Who I should be grateful for. Instead, all I feel is shackled and suffocated.

Pulling out my phone, I open my banking app and ensure that the money transfer went through to Mom earlier today. This is the third transfer I've made in as many weeks, yet she still continues to work herself into the ground, and honestly, it pisses me the fuck off. I've worked my ass off for the last nineteen years to be in this position. To be able to provide for her, the way she provided for me.

I watched her all those years, working shifts around

the clock. Constantly exhausted. And for what? To pay rent on some shithole one-bedroom apartment, where she slept on a fold-out sofa because she refused to let me take it. Putting food on the table for me, while I watched her live off ramen and peanut butter and jelly sandwiches. My mother sacrificed everything for me, and this was supposed to be the pay off. This is what all my hard work was supposed to be for. Instead, she continues to work herself to the bone. And while I managed to talk her into upgrading to a nicer two-bedroom apartment in a better neighborhood, it's still not what I want for her. Unfortunately, it turns out I inherited my stubbornness from my mother.

Sighing, I scrub a hand up and down my face before checking the time. I should let Cassidy know that she can leave, but I can't quite bring myself to do it yet. I would never admit it to anyone, but having her in the office brings an air of lightness. Her quick wit, and even her snarkiness, helps to quell the disquiet I find myself experiencing more often than not.

Turning, I look out my window and take in the New York skyline. Lit up at night, it really is an extraordinary view, and one that I have slowly begun to take for granted. Although that seems to be the theme of my life at the moment.

Snatching up my coffee mug I head out to grab some more caffeine, and figure I'll send Cassidy home on my way. Opening my door, I see that she's not at her desk, but that's not altogether uncommon. The woman honestly has an attention span of a gnat sometimes, and I've learned that allowing her a bit of freedom to goof off occasionally, actually increases her work productivity. Go figure.

Making my way up the hallway, my ears are suddenly assaulted by a loud crashing noise and a string of expletives.

"Stupid, fucking cunt cracker. Ugh, you mother-fucking cunty douchehole. I am going to end you!" Dropping the mug, I race ahead, feeling the adrenaline start to surge at the thought of Cassidy in trouble. My fists are already curling into balls, ready to take out whoever is hurting her. The noises get louder as I approach the copier room, and my heart rate acceler-ates. I throw myself through the doorway only to be met with the sight of Cassidy bent over the copier machine, ass up and swaying high as she smashes the copier with a fist while continuing to berate it.

My body sags as I realize the threat of danger is non-existent; however, as I take in the view in front of me, a smirk plays across my lips, and my dick quickly stands to attention.

With a final curse, Cassidy straightens, and just when I think her tantrum is over, she lays one hell of a kick on the machine before slumping over it dramatically.

"Everything okay in here?" My voice is laced with humor that I don't even bother trying to hide, even though I know it will antagonize her to no end.

Her body tenses at my words, but she doesn't move. "The copier won't work, and I need these copies, and I'm hungry, and today has sucked ass, and you guys have way too many meetings, and it's like you don't even *try* to make them fun. And I really need these copies." She spits this out without taking a breath, and if her tone wasn't filled with defeat, I would be chuckling at her dramatics. Instead, I find myself instinctively moving toward her, the need to comfort the drama queen overwhelming me.

Reaching her, I notice out the corner of my eye that the copier is unplugged. Containing a derisive snort, I lean over to stick the plug back in. I'm ready to give her shit when I feel her move beneath me, and I realize that in the process of fixing her copier woes, I have positioned myself right behind her, our legs pressed up against each other. My dick nestled against her ass. It feels fucking incredible. Then just when I think I have my body under control, her round ass wiggles slightly, as if trying to introduce itself to my cock. I stifle a groan and she stands up, her body now completely flush with mine. My hips intuitively press forward, and I hear a low moan from deep in her throat.

She turns around unexpectedly, and her hand finds my neck, pulling my mouth down to hers. Her tongue invades my mouth with a savagery that seems befitting of Cassidy. There's nothing gentle, or soft about this. It's down-and-dirty mouth fucking. Her hands find my chest and she pushes me backwards. I allow the movement, curious to see where she takes this. Slamming my back into the wall, I smile inwardly. Her fight for dominance is cute. Futile, but cute.

Breaking our kiss, I pull back and look into her eyes. The blue is unique, unlike any I've seen before. A bright cerulean, her eyes echo the complexity of her personality.

"What are you doing, Crazy?"

"Well, Sunshine, I'm pretty sure I'm about to fuck you."

"You don't say? Lucky for you, I'm good with that." Grabbing a handful of her pastel hair, I pull back roughly, exposing her neck. My mouth bites down, and the sound it elicits causes me to bite even harder before I lick the sting away. Moving my attention to her mouth, I lick along her bottom lip while my hands coast along the lines of her body, exploring and tracing every curve; desperate to discover every inch of her. Finding the hem of her skirt, I yank it up in one fluid motion. I kiss her harder, my cock swelling painfully against my zipper as I allow a hand to drop to her pussy. I trace along the red lace panties that have me about ready to blow my load from one glance, before pushing them aside and teasing my middle finger along her slit. She's so fucking wet, it's taking every ounce of my self-control not to push her against the nearest surface and slam into her.

My finger starts thrusting in and out, and she writhes against me, her body showing me what she needs, and I sure as hell am going to give it to her. The noises she's making are undeniably carnal, and when she lifts her leg and wraps it around my waist, opening herself up to me completely, I'm just about done for. Then her hand finds mine, guiding it to her clit and squeezing, her accompanying groan shreds the last bit of my self-control.

I pull my hand away, and grasping her thighs I lift her up and move us quickly toward the copier. Pushing her forcefully on top of the machine, her legs encircle my waist and pull me in so that I can feel the heat of her pussy. As she grinds against me, I close my eyes tight against the sensations she's inciting. Her hands reach for my belt, but they fumble, giving the tiniest hint that she's anxious about what we're doing. I still them and lean back, seeking reassurance that this is what she really wants.

Her eyes narrow under my scrutiny before she pulls my head down and brings those lips that are swollen from my kisses to my ear, and whispers exactly what I want to hear.

"Get your dick out, Sunshine, and fuck me."

Nipping her earlobe, I tug gently before letting my breath whisper across it, relishing her accompanying shiver. "Careful what you wish for, Crazy."

With no further hesitation, I undo my belt and tug my zipper down before Cassidy's hand dives into my boxer briefs and frees my cock which is already straining toward her. Grabbing her wrists, I move them behind her back, and firmly take hold of them with one hand. Using the other hand, I move her panties to the side, and line myself up with her entrance. Then with one hard thrust I slam into her until I am fully seated. I can feel my balls already tightening, and I know this is going to be a quick fuck. Using my thumb to circle her clit, I listen to all her little noises as I continue to slam into her at a frantic pace. Her breathing speeds up, and just as I feel her tightening around my dick, coming for me, her head falls forward, her teeth bite into my shoulder, and I feel her strangled cry muffled into my shirt. Continuing to pound into her relentlessly, I feel my orgasm barrelling through me with an intensity I haven't felt in a long time. It hits me a moment later, her pussy milking every last drop from me, and in a moment of madness my mouth finds her ear again. "I fucking own you."

We slump into each other, our breathing ragged. I release her wrists and my hand moves to her hair, grasping it firmly as my forehead meets her shoulder. Her hands wander under my shirt, teasing the ridges of my abs, and it's as my cock starts to thicken again that sanity returns, and I realize what we just did.

"Fuck," I hiss. "We didn't even use—"

"I'm clean," she interrupts me. "And I'm on the pill. So as long as you're clean, then we're all good."

"I am," I assure her distractedly. My mind is a fucking mess right now. This was a major fuckup on my part. I don't have time for a relationship. And Cassidy isn't the type of woman you can fuck every now and then. She's the type of woman who consumes you.

As I listen to the sound of her breath slow, I try to figure out how best to handle this situation. It can't happen again, for so many reasons, but mainly because it would inevitably end in a fireball of mess and recriminations. I can't be what a woman like her needs, and I suspect when all is said and done, I would be the one with a broken heart. Fuck if I have any self-control with her special brand of crazy, though. If anyone is going to keep this relationship platonic, it's going to have to be her. And I can only think of one way to make sure that happens.

My forehead rests on her shoulder, and I close my eyes in an effort to protect myself from what I am about to do to her.

"So, do you fuck all your bosses on the photocopier, or did I catch you at an especially low moment?" I bite this out, injecting every ounce of venom I can into that sentence, while my chest tightens painfully. I feel her entire body tense at the sound of my words before she roughly pushes me away.

"Are you fucking kidding me, Sunshine? Are you actually pulling your prick pants on while your dick is still nestled in my pussy, and your cum is dripping down my thighs? Is that what's happening right now?"

Breaking our connection, she hops off the copier before removing her panties, and using them to clean herself up. Tucking myself away, I watch her, careful to keep my eyes impassive.

Turning to face me, those eyes I was admiring just twenty minutes earlier, are now full of hostility. "I'm sure there's nothing else I can do for you, so I'm going to head home now, *Mr. Alexander*." Her voice drips with disdain, and I inwardly cringe.

"I'll see you tomorrow." I attempt to sound as professional as possible, but it's hard to play the proper boss when you just fucked, and then dismissed, your assistant in less time than it takes to watch an episode of *Arrested Development*.

Cassidy's eyes flicker with something I can't decipher. Something I'd give my left nut to be able to figure out. Then just like that her eyes clear, the sneer disappears, and she flashes me a bright smile.

"Later, gator."

And as she struts out of the room with a dignity I wouldn't have thought possible, it dawns on me. She's going to make me suffer for this moment of weakness.

CHAPTER SEVEN

CASSIDY

"Kimberly!" I plop my ass on her desk as Kim regards me suspiciously.

"Yes?"

"You free for lunch? Tanya's coming down to go over some files with me. I figured we could try to make it somewhat enjoyable by making it a girls' lunch and adding some cocktails to the mix. You in?"

"Sure, sounds good. I'll ask Rachel too."

"The more the merrier, babes."

"We should try that new—" Kim's face twists comically as she stares at something over my shoulder, a look of curious fear alighting her features. Twisting slightly, I glance back and spot Mason storming down the hallway, his glare fixed on me. *Shit.*

"Gotta go." Jumping off the desk, I race down the corridor as fast as these devil heels will take me, and throw myself into my chair. I snatch up the phone receiver in a race to occupy myself before Mason arrives, but much to my dismay, a large hand grabs it from me, and slams it into the base.

"Good morning, Mr. Alexander, how was your meeting this morning?" I force every bit of sweetness I can muster into that sentence.

"Fine," he spits out through clenched teeth. "I want you in my office. Now."

Fuckfuckfuckfuckfuckfuck. It's been three weeks since his fuck and run, and I have spent those weeks making him pay for that humiliation and enjoying every second of it. How exactly have I been torturing the delectable dastard? You know, the usual stuff. Wallpapering his office with pictures of Justin Bieber. In his underwear. Booby trapping his chair. And my personal favorite; hiding a small tape recorder in his office that played the sound of a toilet flushing every thirty minutes. The volume was set so it could just barely be heard. I swear I thought he was going to have a nervous breakdown trying to figure out where it was coming from. Yeah, that was a good day.

But even I had to admit that I might have crossed a line yesterday.

I make my way into the lion's den as slowly as possible; I have a feeling that this isn't going to end well for me. Looking up, I see Mason is already seated at his desk.

"A happy ending, Cassidy? Seriously?" I scowl at him with an intensity that surprises even me. I know that I'm in the wrong here, I really do, but his tone of righteous indignation tickles my bitch bunny, and she wants to come out and play.

"Are you offering, Sunshine? Because, really, been there, done that, and all I got was some lousy cum-stained panties to show for it." A fleeting look of something that resembles pain crosses his face, causing me a moment of regret. That is, until the memory of trying desperately to hold onto my dignity as I walked away with his cum dripping down my thighs overwhelms me.

"My massage. What was supposed to be a *remedial* massage. Sound familiar?"

"Yes, Mr. Alexander. I made the appointment myself. Was there a problem?" His eyes widen, as if he can't believe my audacity. But really, I've been working here for how long now? He should know me better than that.

"No, there was no problem at all. Until she insisted on massaging my dick, and wouldn't take no for an answer. I actually had to pay her *not* to suck me off."

"Was that a change of pace for you? More used to it being the other way around, huh?"

Mason is practically vibrating with rage at my words, and if I didn't hate him so much right now, I might be able to admit that pissed off is a good look on him. But I do, so I won't.

"Cassidy." His shoulders slump, and it's as if saying my name has broken him. "You crossed a line. That was just… too far."

He's right. Of course he's right. And I wish I could apologize to him. But that would mean acknowledging how much he hurt me. And I wasn't about to admit that the first man since Aidan to ignite any feeling in me, had in turn, made me feel like nothing.

"I'll pack my things and be out of here in fifteen minutes."

I move to leave, but before I can take more than two steps, Mason's startled voice stops me.

"What? I didn't fire you, Cassidy." Sighing, he pinches the bridge of his nose between his fingertips, grimacing. "Can we maybe just agree to no more practical jokes involving my cock? Maybe stick to things like replacing the cream in my donut with mayo, okay?"

I can't control the smile that explodes across my face. I had forgotten about that little trick.

"Yeah, I guess I can make that work." Shrugging nonchalantly, I ignore the fluttering in my belly.

"Good. Now get back to work, Crazy."

Giving him a mock salute, I make my way back to my desk. Don't ask me why, but I may also add a little extra sway to my sashay.

"You did what?!"

"Oh my god, how are you not fired?"

"I'm sure the fucker deserved it."

Looking around the table, I take in the shocked expressions. Well, Kim and Rachel's shocked expressions. Tanya's could more accurately be described as gleeful.

"In my defence, I never actually believed there

would be any touching involved. I totally thought he would figure it out before that. Can I really be blamed for his lack of attention to detail? I don't think so." To punctuate my point, I take a big slurp of my mudslide. Day drinking really is the best.

"I can't believe he didn't fire you. He's such a moody fucker. I've never met a man that terrifies me, and turns me on in equal measure. I honestly don't know how you two work with him." Kim wiggles a finger between Tanya and I.

"I have to admit he's getting worse." Tanya sighs. "He's always been a total workaholic, but it was always tempered with a sense of fun, you know? We could always have a laugh, but lately he's been like a bear with a sore head. If he's not careful, I'm finally going to give him that ass kicking I'm always threatening."

"Maybe he needs to get laid?" Rachel waggles her eyebrows at us as she takes a sip of her Midori illusion, and I almost spit my drink out.

"I don't know, he's not too bad when I'm working with him." I shrug, unsure why I'm defending the dickhole.

"Really?" Tanya draws the word out while eyeing me up and down in a manner that I find all kinds of exposing. Time for a subject change.

"How's the baby?"

Tanya's face immediately softens. "She's perfect. She's just started sleeping through the night, thank God. For a while there I had Reagan waking for feeds during the night, as well as Trinidy up a couple of times a night with nightmares. It was horrific."

"I remember going through that with my girls. The twins were awful. As soon as Sienna went down, Harper would wake up. It was like they had made a pact that one of them must be awake at all times. I really thought I would lose my mind at one point." Rachel frowns at the memory.

"I got really lucky, Madelyn was a wonderful sleeper as a baby," Kim chimes in, before grimacing. "She's making up for it now though."

Talk around the table turns to all things kids, husbands, and general domestic drudgery. I lean back in my chair, inhaling my drink far quicker than I should, especially considering I still have an afternoon of work ahead of me.

It's moments like these, though, that I struggle with. Moments where it slaps me up the side of the head just how different my life could be right now. If my life hadn't been torn apart by one moment of horror. Maybe Aidan and I would be married right now. Maybe we would have a couple of chubby babies that I could squish to my heart's content.

Or maybe we would have ended. Weeks, months, or even years later. For the first time, it occurs to me that maybe he wasn't my forever.

An hour later, I am on autopilot as I make my way slowly back to the office. The pounding in my head is hard and fast, and if I was feeling better I might be capable of making some sly innuendo about the correlation between that and my fucking preference.

Hearing my phone buzz, I pull it out of my purse, and my whole body sags in relief when I see the name on the screen. *Skye. Thank the sweet lord Channing Tatum for Skye.* Walking into the lobby of Cook Enterprises, I take a seat on one of the elegant feather-gray chaises in the seating area. Checking my watch, I note that I am already ten minutes late back to work, but Sunshine will just have to deal.

Skye: Drinks tonight?

Cassidy*:* Babes, I have had a life-altering epiphany over lunch. So, yeah, drinks tonight.

Skye: WHAT?!?!

My hand tightens around my phone. I haven't told Skye what happened with Mason, yet. I'm not sure why. I'd like to think it was for some noble reason like I didn't want to put her in an awkward position, what with Mason being her boyfriend's best friend. But the truth is, I think I'm more scared that I'll have to face the fact that I'm not her person anymore, Ben is, and if she's forced to choose, I could lose my best friend. I need her though, so pulling on my big girl panties I rip off the bandaid.

Cassidy: I fucked Mason.

Skye: Cassidy Jensen I am going to KILL YOU!!!

Cassidy: If it helps, Balls, he pretty much blew me off while his dick was still inside of me.

Skye: I am going to fucking KILL HIM!!!!

Cassidy: There you go. Welcome back to the light side. Maybe Mae's at 7?

Skye: I'll be there.

Skye: Cass?

Cassidy: Yeah?

Skye: I love you.

Rushing through the door, my eyes scan the crowded bar searching for Skye. Which is easier said than done, since she's a total shortass, and is easily lost in a crowd. Finally spotting her extended arm waving madly over in the corner, I motion toward the bar to let her know that I'm going to grab a drink on my way through to her. Shaking her head, she holds up a cocktail she must have snagged for me, and my mouth waters at the sight of the chocolatey alcoholic goodness she is proffering.

I push my way through the crowd. It's rowdy tonight and I'm not really in the mood to deal with drunk assholes. At least not until I'm one of them.

Finally reaching the table, my hand immediately goes for the drink, but Skye grabs it out of my reach before my fingertips even graze it.

"What the fuck, Balls?" She scrunches up her nose at the term of endearment I know she hates.

"Nope. Sit." Pointing her finger at the chair, Skye has her hardass look firmly in place. She's so fucking adorable.

"Fine." Taking a seat, I prepare myself for the inquisition that is sure to follow.

"Spill, Jensen. When I am satisfied, you'll get your drink."

"Well damn, Skyeballs, I thought you had Spanky to keep you satisfied these days, but if he's failing in his manly duties, then I'm happy to help out." Waggling my eyebrows at her, I take great delight in her small shriek of horror.

"Ben is more than keeping me satisfied, thank you very much. In fact, last night he did this thing with his…" She pauses, and even in the dark bar I can see the blush that flushes her cheeks.

"Finish that sentence, Skye Emery. Finish that fucking sentence."

She giggles, and brings her Pina colada to her lips. "Later. After some more of these," she replies, raising her glass with another giggle. Right then I vow to get Skyeballs fucking sloshed tonight. I love her sordid Spanky sex tales. Who would have ever thought a goof-ball like Ben could sink the sausage like a porn star?

"So, you and Mason?" My shoulders slump at her question. Me and Mason. Is there a me and Mason? Nope.

"We fucked. It was a mistake. Which he made very clear before his dick had even left Princess's warm embrace. That's it."

"Ugh, you need to stop referring to your vajayjay by name, Cass. It's not normal." I snort out a laugh. Little does she know, the day she stops being horrified, is the day I'll stop calling my fingerhut Princess.

"Explain better, Cassidy. I still feel clueless."

Sighing deeply, I turn imploring eyes on her. "Please

let me have a little sip first? I need it, Skye, I neeeeeeed it." She rolls her eyes at my dramatics before reluctantly handing over my mudslide. Taking a less than dainty slurp, I close my eyes and try to figure out where to start.

"I want to fuck him all the time. Like, *all. The. Time.* Pretty much anytime he makes eye contact I'm ready to drop to my knees and blow." Skye almost chokes on her drink at my confession, and I thump her on her back until she can breathe again.

"Okay, well what's the problem then? It's not like you to get twisted up over some guy. This is a temporary job, yeah? Have some fun. I honestly can't imagine Mason being an asshole, not on purpose anyway. He's probably just under a lot of stress and doesn't realize how he's coming off. Talk to him. Let him know he crossed a line, and then let him know how he can make it up to you, nudge nudge, wink wink." And just in case I couldn't infer her meaning, she nudges me, and winks a couple of times. My face freezes in horror. Both at her nerdiness, and in confusion. Because it's not that easy.

"He asked me if I fuck all my bosses. While he was still in me. So, yeah, I don't think it's that easy."

Skye's face contorts into a look of rage unlike any I have seen before. "I am going to fucking cut his balls off!" she shrieks as she pulls her phone out of her purse. Making a mad grab for the cell, I ask her what she's doing, my voice tinged with desperation. "I'm going to tell the fucker off! He's dead to me, Cass. *Dead!*"

"Okay, calm your tits, Balls, and stop." Ignoring me she continues to type away. *"Stop!"*

Something in my tone must get her attention, because her fingers stop racing across the keyboard, and she slowly places the phone on the table in front of her, her eyes scanning my face while my heart starts to slow its frantic pace.

"What's going on, Cass? You don't put up with shit like that. That was a dick move to pull. Jesus, he deserves to *lose* his dick for that. Honestly, I'm surprised you didn't cut it off." She points her drink at me, as she continues. "If you ever reconsider that, I will happily hunt down a pair of scissors, and hold him down for you." A smile flits across my face at this very un-Skye-like statement. Then her eyes soften, and she reaches across the table to grasp my hand.

"Talk to me."

"I can't stop thinking about him." I say this as if it's a sin I need to confess. "And yes, he's hot, and I would like to play hide the salami with him again. Because his salami is big, Balls, like *big* big, and he's really good at hiding it. But it's also that he talks to his Mom regularly, and wants to take care of her. It's that, after overhearing one of the receptionists talk about her son, he sent them the entire Harry Potter book series, because she's a single mom and she mentioned that he had asked for them, but she couldn't afford them. It's that he orders Krispy Kreme donuts for the office because they're my favorites. Even though I *know* that he prefers Dunkin' Donuts." The word vomit is spewing out of me at an alarming rate, but I can't seem to stop.

"It's that every time he's an asshole, there's a moment where he looks as though he wants to dickpunch himself for acting that way. It's that I want to know what he's thinking pretty much constantly." I pause, breathless. "It's that he's the first man that I've ever wanted to want me."

Eyes wide, Skye considers my epic speech before responding. "It's that way, huh?" A smile lights up her whole face. "You know what you've got, Cassidy Jensen?"

"What? What do I have, Skye Emery?"

"Feelings! You caught feelings! I knew it would happen one day. I feel so freaking vindicated right now, you have no idea."

"Jesus, you're practically giddy, I have had feelings before, you know." I try to temper my tone, but I'm kind of offended right now.

"I know you have, Cass, but not like this, right? This is next level. I'm excited for you!"

"Well, don't get too excited. Nothing can happen until he gets over his cunt complex, which I don't see happening anytime soon."

"How much longer do you think you'll be working there? To be honest I thought he would have found a permanent replacement ages ago."

"Yeah, so did I. He interviews a couple of people a week, but he finds fault with all of them. I'm not complaining though. The pay is decent, and the hours have been working really well for me." Grabbing my cocktail, I take a huge sip before continuing. "Did I tell you that Mason gave me some freelance catering work? He orders a dozen cupcakes for every business meeting. I've actually made a few contacts because of it." She eyes me up and down.

"So, I guess he has a cutie complex to rival his C-U-N-T one, huh?"

I roll my eyes hard at this. "Seriously?" Her only response is a giggle as she drains the rest of her drink.

"Okay, so. Essentially, you have feelings for him, but it's too complicated, so you need to get over him? At least until he realizes what's staring him in the face, and comes to his senses. Yeah?"

"Yeah." I shrug. "I guess if you break it down, I need to figure out how to work with him, without mounting him on a piece of office equipment, again."

"How did you feel when he asked you if you had fucked all your bosses?"

"Uh, like I wanted to literally kill him. In the most deliciously painful way imaginable. Something involving a machete sounded good." My eyes light up at the thought. "But then that passed, and I was hurt. And embarrassed that he would think that about me. It was fucking humiliating."

"I want you to remember that feeling every time he makes your heart flutter. Or your beaver flutter. *Especially* when he makes your beaver flutter! Remember how mortified you felt, and then throat punch him. Simple!"

"Simple, hey? No, you're right. I can definitely shut it down if I just keep remembering that moment. But maybe I'll skip the throat punching though. I want to hold onto this job."

"Right, good plan."

Feeling my shoulders relax, I motion to the waitress so we can get another round of drinks. "So, tell me about this magical thing Spanky did last night. I want to hear all about it." Skye's answering giggle eases the last of my tension, and I settle in to hear all about Ben's wicked ways.

The next day, I hurry my hungover ass to the office, hopeful that maybe Mason won't notice my lateness. Despite my pounding head and tired eyes, I'm feeling more hopeful after my talk with Skye last night. I can get my shit on lockdown and make this work. I have to.

My hopes of sneaking in unnoticed are dashed when, opening the door to our offices, I find Mason leaning over my desk, staring intently at my computer monitor.

"You alright there, Sunshine? If it helps, my plot to take you down isn't on there. It's all saved up here." I tap my temple. As I walk closer, I see that he has his schedule pulled up.

"I'll keep that in mind." His tone is droll. "Look, I have some bad news. I need to head to Seattle for some emergency meetings. We'll probably be there a few days, and we'll need to leave tomorrow, so if you can book flights now, please."

Switching into work mode, I pick up the phone receiver ready to make the call.

"Business class tomorrow morn— wait, did you say

we?" My hand has stopped midway to my ear as realization dawns on me. His eyes are apologetic as they meet mine.

"I'm sorry, but I need my assistant there, and Tanya can't come on such short notice."

Refusing to let him see how much this is affecting me, I bring the receiver to my ear and start dialling. "No problem."

Motherfucker.

CHAPTER EIGHT

MASON

"Thank you for your time, Charles. We'll take these revisions back to our team, and see if we can put together a proposal that meets all of your expectations." I do my very best to keep my voice level, despite the overwhelming need to punch something right about now. Preferably Alistair Thompson. However, since the dickwad couldn't be fucked turning up for the meetings *he* requested, instead sending his minions, that would prove to be difficult.

After shaking hands, and exchanging some inconsequential small talk, I finally make my way out of the conference room with Cassidy right at my heels. As if dealing with all this business bullshit hasn't been stressful enough, having her right by my side for ten hours a day is proving to be my biggest challenge. The scent of her sweet perfume is constantly irritating my nose; she smells like a goddamn cupcake anytime of the day. It's a constant reminder of how good she smelt when my face was buried in her neck, and my dick was buried in her pussy.

Giving my head a slight shake to clear the images that seem to haunt me, I hone in on the sound of Cassidy's voice, and realize that she's talking to that asshole, Marshall, who has been eyeing her off like a fucking dog in heat for the past three days.

"I would kill for a decent burger right now, the ones from room service are pretentious crap." She's practically salivating at the thought.

"There's this great burger place not far from here, it's a local favorite. If you have time why don't we go and grab some dinn—"

"We have plans tonight," I cut the dickless loser off. "We have work to go over." Cassidy's gaze slowly washes over me, a knowing look in her eye. I have no fucking idea how I'm going to play this off with her, but I also couldn't care less right now.

"Oh. Well, okay." Marshall seems thoroughly unconvinced, and he looks between Cassidy and I suspiciously before shrugging. "Good seeing you again, man." He offers me his hand. "And, Cassidy, it was great meeting you. Maybe if you're ever this way again, we can grab that burger." Marshall side eyes me as he says this. *Motherfucker*. "Have a good night, guys, don't work too hard." With a wink that cements his douche status, he heads off in the opposite direction, leaving me alone with the woman of my dreams. Or nightmares. Depending on the time of day.

"Work, huh?" Her tone drips with sarcasm.

"I figured you needed saving. You can thank me later."

"Yes. I definitely needed saving from the tall, sexy piece of man meat who would have bought me a great burger, and then most likely fucked me hard and fast in his ostentatious-single-rich-guy car. Oh, thank you, sweet savior."

"You're welcome." Choosing to ignore her tone of irony, as well as the sudden anger that image ignites, I continue, "I actually know the place he was talking about. If you want to, we could head over and grab something?"

Her eyes light up, and my dick twitches at the promise they hold. Just as quickly, however, they shutter and her head shakes slightly.

"That's probably not a good idea, Mason." Her voice holds regret, and I know if I pushed I could convince her to agree. But I also know that's probably not what is best for either of us. So, instead, I nod my head in agreeance, and give her a forced smile.

We make our way down the corridor in silence, distancing ourselves from the room we've been locked in for the past three days. For the first time I am grateful that these meetings were held in the hotel where we are staying. When the elevator appears up ahead, I let out a small sigh of relief. In about three minutes I'll be in my hotel room, away from temptation. I can order some dinner, then pull up Porn Hub and relieve a bit of tension before turning in for the night. I make a promise to myself that this time, it won't be Cassidy's face I imagine as I come all over my hand.

In a moment of serendipity, the doors to the elevator open just as we step up to it, and as we walk inside I feel tension coiling in my shoulders. Being in such a confined space with Cassidy challenges my self-control.

Pushing the button to our floor, the atmosphere is almost suffocating, and I know she can feel it too. The lack of smartass comments being thrown my way is a good indicator. I turn slightly and take in her profile. She really is fucking sexy. That pink hair falls over her shoulders in soft waves, and I can't help but notice it's the perfect length to wrap around my fist. Her blue eyes are wide, surrounded by dark lashes and her nose is delicate, perfectly in proportion. But it's her mouth that catches my attention. Full lips, that I have imagined wrapped around my cock more times than I care to admit.

She turns and catches me staring. I can see her mind ticking over, and I find myself leaning forward, waiting to hear whatever shit she's going to give me. Her mouth opens, but before she can get anything out there is a loud crash and the elevator comes to a grinding halt. The lights flicker briefly, and Cassidy's hand finds mine and clings to it before falling away as soon as the light stabilizes.

We look at each other in shocked silence. "Are you fucking kidding me?" Her voice resonates with a mix of disbelief and annoyance. "What do we do now?" I pick up on the slight waver in her voice, and immediately switch into get-shit-done mode.

"We let someone know what's happened, and then wait while they get us out of here. It shouldn't take long." She nods her agreement, and I keep my eyes trained on her as I pick up the emergency telephone, and then talk to building maintenance. When I'm done, she rolls her eyes and huffs out in unfettered exasperation. Fucked if I know what I've done though.

"You going to elaborate on that 'hmph,' or am I supposed to know what the attitude is for?"

"How long are we going to be stuck in here?" She ignores my question, her tone curt.

"He said it should be about twenty minutes. Now are you going to tell me what bug crawled up your ass, or not?"

Her eyes narrow, and if looks could kill I'd be burning in hell right about now. Damned if it wouldn't be a hell of a way to go, though.

"You're kind of an asshole, you know that?" I do know that, but I'm not going to give her the satisfaction of agreeing with her.

"Why am I an asshole today, Crazy?"

"You were rude to whoever you were talking to! It's not their fault we're stuck in here." Her face is scrunched up with a look of distaste, and she looks about ready to hurl more insults my way.

I fucking own you. Those words have been burned into my consciousness since the night they fell out of my mouth, and it's moments like this, when she's feisty and doing her damndest to put me in my place, that I wish they were true.

I move forward subconsciously, invading her space so that I am all she can feel.

"That wasn't rude. That was direct. There's a difference."

Her eyes search mine; I'm not sure what she's looking for, but whatever she finds seems to satisfy her. Still, she takes a step back, moving away from me.

"You could still be nicer." Her voice is strong, and I have to admit I respect her for never backing down. Even if she is wrong.

I follow her path, taking a step forward and leaning down so she is forced to meet my gaze. "Nice gets you nothing in this life, Crazy." The small strangled noise she makes in denial causes my dick to harden, and it takes every ounce of self-control I have to move away from her, allowing us both space to breathe. "Besides, it was building maintenance, so yeah, they are kind of responsible."

Sighing, Cassidy throws her huge-ass purse to the floor and slides down the wall until she is sitting next to it. Looking up, she motions for me to do the same. "May as well make yourself comfortable if we're going to be here for a while."

Moving to the other side of the elevator, I take a seat facing her. She is openly scrutinising me, her stare appraising, and making me fucking uncomfortable. I reach for my tie and loosen it, undoing the top buttons of my shirt and then rolling my shirt sleeves up to my elbows. Her eyes immediately fall to my right arm, taking in the tattoos that cover my forearm, and I realize that in all the time we've worked together she's never seen them. Her tongue peeks out and glides along her bottom lip before her teeth bite down; the sight reminding me of the way she bit into my shoulder the moment she came.

"What's that about?" she asks, pointing to my sleeve. "The artwork kind of clashes with your asshole businessman persona, doesn't it?" Her eyes widen, and she claps her hands together, suddenly gleeful. "Oh my god, do you have a secret bad-boy past, Sunshine? Is that what this is?"

I throw my head back with a loud laugh. "No, no secret bad-boy past. I'm sorry to disappoint."

Her delight is replaced with a look of curiosity. Waving a finger at me, she asks, "So you've always been like *this* then?"

"*This?*"

"Yeah, serious. Responsible." Her lips lift in a smile full of mischief. "Asshole-ish."

Her words are light, and I know she's joking, but it reminds me of the role I was compelled to play. How quickly I was forced to grow up, and it pisses me off. But before I can reply she continues.

"I mean, you have to admit, you're kind of a freak. You work around the clock, I never see any social events on your calendar unless they're work related. You're a CEO for Christ's sake! What kind of twenty-nine-year-old is a fucking CEO So, yeah, I'm thinking you were always an anal retentive, control freak." She pauses briefly to take a breath before throwing the knockout punch. "No wonder you have to fuck your secretary on the copier." She looks away, refusing to make eye contact, and I feel the anger start to simmer. I'm pretty good at shutting my emotions down. I've been blocking out that bullshit for almost twenty years. But hearing her belittle what happened between us, when I've been doing everything I can to deny this pull I have to her, causes me to snap and lash out.

"No. I was your typical kid, until my father went to prison when I was ten. I had to grow up pretty fucking quickly after that." I plough on, not giving her a chance to interrupt. "And I have no trouble getting laid, but what man would turn down a piece of ass when it's wiggled in his face?" Even I can hear the bitterness in my voice, and I immediately regret both my confession, and the attack on her.

I watch as her eyes widen, her fists clench and her entire body seems to start vibrating with rage. Then just as suddenly as her physical reaction started, it stops, and she slumps, closing her eyes.

When they open they seek mine, and are full of empathy. "Your father went to prison? What for? Shit, your poor mom."

"Mom was better off without the bastard." My voice comes out harsher than I intended, and I notice her flinch. Adjusting my tone, I continue, "he wasn't a good guy. I think it was probably the best thing that could have happened."

"That must have been hard, though. Your mom is a nurse, yeah?"

"How do you even know that?" I ask with a small grin.

"We talk, obviously. Your mom is far more likeable than you, fyi." She throws me a smirk that calms me down, and I feel my body relax.

"I don't know what you're talking about, according to Mom I'm the most charming man in the world." Her answering laugh is loud and reckless. It makes me want to prove that I can be just as reckless.

"Well, then Rhonda is a damn liar!" She wipes her eyes, as her laughter subsides, and I can't help but return her smile.

"I couldn't even imagine not having my dad around, so I'm sorry that happened. Even if it was for the better, that doesn't mean it was easy."

"It wasn't. Mom worked all the time just to make enough money to survive. I mean, it wasn't much better before the prick went away, but after, it was almost unbearable." Cassidy watches me intently, nibbling on her bottom lip, and I feel a surge of protectiveness. The instinct to make her a part of my life is getting harder to fight. In an effort to distract myself, I continue. "I used to wake up some mornings just as she was getting home from work. She would be so tired she wouldn't even be able to stay awake through breakfast, no matter how hard she tried. I decided that one day I would make enough money that she would never have to work again, and I've worked my ass off to make sure that happened."

"Well, that's all very noble, Sunshine, but some women don't want a man providing for them, you know. Considering your mom still works, I would say she falls into that category, right?" I have to stifle a snort at that. She has definitely got my mother figured out.

I think back to all of the arguments we had when I was younger. My mom always encouraging me to 'follow my bliss' or some shit like that, rather than supporting my goal to follow the money train.

"Right. She never really got on board with the plan."

"Do you ever regret it? The hours you put in, everything you missed out on to achieve an unachievable goal?" Her voice is softer now. "You deserve more than a late-night fuck on a piece of office equipment, Mason." She meets my eye, challenging me. "So do I."

I feel as though she just sucker punched me with those three words. But she's right.

"Yeah, you do, Crazy." My hands find my hair and tug carelessly as I try to figure out how to make her understand. "I don't have time for a relationship, Cassidy. It wouldn't be fair to start something I can't make a priority."

I take her in as she considers my words. She's twirling a lock of hair around her finger with an unreadable look on her face, and in that moment, I realize how much trouble I'm in. Because as much as the desire to fuck her consumes me, the bigger danger is how much I like her.

She's passionate and intelligent, and even though she expresses it in the most unorthodox ways, her heart is as big as her mouth.

She brings a lightness to my life that it's lacking,

and I cling to it every time she walks away. And make no mistake, she will always walk away. A man like me could never be enough for a woman like her.

"You know what I think?" She quirks an eyebrow at me, almost daring me to deny her. "I think that's complete bullshit." Her eyes light up with defiance, and she crosses her legs, leaning forward. "You have the best possible team working under you, but you refuse to delegate anything of significance. There's absolutely no reason why you need to be at the office sixteen hours *every day*, as well as spending weekends there. I think you use your work as an excuse to avoid living."

I open my mouth to defend myself, but immediately clamp it shut. Because she might possibly have a point. Cassidy's face is animated as she continues.

"Any woman that matters is going to understand that you have a demanding job, but as long as you're always making an effort to put her first whenever you can, that will be enough. Loving her is the most important thing. You do that, and you're gold."

Her words make their intended impact, and in an effort to deflect, I turn the tables on her.

"What about you? From what I hear, you're not really into relationships either."

"Aw, have you been asking about me, Sunshine?" She holds her hand over her heart, in a faux swoon. "I'm so flattered!"

Not prepared to let her off the hook, I persist. "No, seriously. You called me on my shit, now it's your turn." I can tell I've pissed her off, her expression turns indignant in the blink of an eye.

"I do relationships. I just only do them with people who deserve the gloriousness that is me. And I haven't found anyone who does since—" she cuts herself off and her eyes widen.

"Since who?" My voice is urgent. I want to know about whoever this dipshit is.

"My college boyfriend."

"Your college boyfriend?" I can't hide my disbelief. "No man has lived up to a *boy*friend you had, what? Ten years ago?" I immediately regret my tone, as I watch her withdraw into herself.

"He was special." Despite her posture, her voice is defiant, and I find myself feeling jealous of this unknown asshole.

"If he's so incredible then why did you break up?"

Cassidy starts wringing her hands in her lap, and her teeth find her bottom lip once again. "We didn't."

Her statement pulls me up short, and I'm momentarily confused. "What does that mean?"

"He died." Her hands stop twisting and she lays them flat on the ground beside her, as if trying to steady herself. Well, fuck.

We sit in silence for a few minutes while I try to fight my instinct to comfort her. I give up. I stand and move beside her, where I take a seat, and gently take her hand in mine, intertwining our fingers. "I'm sorry."

"It was a long time ago. He was in a car accident." She lays her head on my shoulder. "I have tried, you know. I loved him, and I know how lucky I was, but I want that kind of love in my life again." She sighs, and her palpable sadness causes a painful ache in my chest.

"I'm beginning to think that lightning doesn't strike twice though."

This statement gives me a moment of pause. "Isn't that good though? Lightning striking kind of sounds like a bad thing." She lifts her head and I turn to see her looking at me incredulously.

"Haven't you ever seen *Sweet Home Alabama*?"

I roll my eyes before replying. "Can't say that I have."

"Uh, well, you *should*! Josh Lucas is totally fuck-worthy in that movie."

"And that is how I decide on my movie viewing. By how fuckworthy the lead actor is."

"Ugh, whatever. Anyone who's seen that film knows that lightning strikes can create true beauty. It's what we should all be holding out for." Her head finds my shoulder again, and as an easy silence falls over us, my lips find her forehead and place a gentle kiss.

"I like you, Mason." Her voice is small, but confident. "And I'm scared. The last time I went all in with someone, I got crushed. The idea of letting someone in like that again, just to lose them, terrifies me. But I can't keep fighting how I feel about you, and I'm kind of sick of trying." She inhales deeply, her body shuddering slightly. "So maybe we start acting like the grown-ups we're supposed to be, and give this thing a go?"

"Are you suggesting I man up, Crazy?" Cassidy snorts out a laugh at my question.

"Fuck no. I'm suggesting you woman up, Sunshine." Her smile is huge, and there is a light in her eyes that I haven't seen before. A light that I want to see every damn day. I'm so fucking done trying to resist her.

I lean down and place my forehead against hers.

"Work could be a problem. I am your boss, and this would be breaking all kinds of rules." I close my eyes, waiting for her response, and hoping she doesn't back off. But when I open them, she's looking at me mischievously.

"You mean it would be," she lowers her voice to a whisper, "*taboo*? Just like Skyeballs' dirty books!" She cackles out a laugh.

Unable to hold myself back, I slant my mouth over hers, and slip my tongue inside, enjoying her shocked moan. My tongue slides against hers before pulling back and I bite down on her bottom lip. The noise she makes is like a lightning bolt to my dick, and my self-control snaps. Pulling her across so that she is straddling my lap, my hand lands on her neck, tracing the gentle slope while she reaches for my belt buckle, our mouths never parting.

The feel of her pussy grinding against my hardened cock is making my head fog. Wrapping my arms around her waist, I stand, taking her with me. I push her against the wall as my fingers deftly work the zip on her pants, and when my hand slips into her panties, I slide two fingers through her slit and tease her clit. She pulls away with a gasp, her mouth open, her eyes rolling back in pleasure.

But just as we get in a rhythm, her pussy pushing back against my palm, desperately seeking release, the elevator shudders and comes back to life, moving us up toward our rooms.

We both still, and my eyes snap to hers where I see my frustration mirrored.

"Don't go getting any ideas, Mr. Alexander, you have a job to finish when we get to my room." She captures my lip with her teeth, and bites down before pulling away and straightening her clothes.

"Looking forward to it, Miss. Jensen." I bring my fingers to her mouth, lightly tracing her lips and coating them with a light sheen of her arousal before stealing a final kiss. Fuck me, she tastes good.

Once we've fixed our clothes, I grab her hand and drag her close to the doors so we can make a run for it as soon as they open. Never before have I been so eager to have my head buried between a woman's thighs.

"Easy there, Sunshine. We have all night." Looking down at her, I see humor glinting in her blue eyes.

"Yeah, and we're going to need every second for what I have planned." I smirk at her excited expression, and when the doors open I drag her through.

We don't have a moment to lose.

CHAPTER NINE

CASSIDY

I glare out the plane's small window, listening to Mason as he talks on his cell beside me. I am frustrated as hell after we were interrupted before we even got started last night. The shrill ring of his phone interrupted us as we hustled back to the hotel room, and he was drawn into a seemingly endless parade of important calls.

I left Mason to it and took care of myself, like every woman should be able to do. But when you've been promised dick, and not just any dick, but the dick of all dicks, well then, a bit of porn and my BOB just didn't cut it. Princess was *not* a happy pussy.

The pilot's announcement asking us to turn off our phones and electronics sounds, and Mason ends his call, lifting his ass slightly so he can pocket his phone.

Since we are flying home on a Saturday, he is dressed casually, and this is the first time I have seen him out of business wear. His legs are encased in a pair of old worn-in faded jeans, that mould to his ass perfectly. And yeah, I was totally checking him out. His outfit is completed with a black Foo Fighters t-shirt that stretches over his broad shoulders, and a pair of black Chucks. The shirt gives me an opportunity to examine his ink, and my eyes trace over the intricate swirls of the tribal design that covers his forearm. The claws of what looks to be some kind of bird peeks out from under his sleeve, and I find myself wishing I could reach over and yank it up to see what he has hiding underneath. Basically, he looks sexy as fuck, and thoughts of joining the mile-high club are playing across my mind, when his deep voice interrupts me.

"I'm sorry about last night." His face holds nothing but sincerity. "It was fucking bad timing. This Thompson guy is a pain in my ass. If this account wasn't going to generate so much income for the company, I wouldn't be putting up with all his shit."

Mason's eyes are tired, and I reach up and stroke my hand along his cheek. He leans into my touch, closing his eyes.

"He sounds like a bit of a cock muncher." His eyes pop open at my statement, and I can see the humor they hold.

"A cock muncher?"

"Well nobody likes a cock muncher, yeah? Those things require a certain finesse, and teeth are generally frowned upon."

His laugh is loud and wonderful, making me tingle in all the good places. He doesn't laugh much, and that thought makes me sad. I make a promise to myself to change that.

"How much sleep did you get last night, Sunshine? You look tired."

"Not much. I think it was after two by the time I finished dealing with shit. It was too late to bother you, so I jerked off, had a couple of drinks, and then turned in."

"Me too! Well, I drank first and then flicked the bean, 'cause that shit makes me sleepy." I hold my fist out to him for a fist bump, but he just looks at it bewildered.

"You want me to fist bump you because we both had to get ourselves off?" He's looking at me as if I'm crazy, so I quickly lower my hand.

"Pfft, your loss."

The flight attendant makes her way down the small aisle with the drinks cart, and we both grab a water, while I also snatch up a bag of honey roasted peanuts. These little fuckers make flying totally worth it.

"So, we should probably talk about the work thing. If we do do this, we'll have to keep it a secret. Is that going to be a problem?"

I'm struggling to open my nuts, and only listening to him with one ear. I seriously don't know what he's so worried about. Secrecy will only make this hotter.

"Yeah, it's fine." I finally pop the bag open, spilling some in the process. Mason picks up a few stray nuts from his lap and hands them to me, drawing my eyes to him. "It's not like I'm going to be working there forever, you have more interviews lined up this week. You might actually find someone who can meet your bizarrely high standards. I honestly don't know why it's taken you so long." I shake my head in exasperation. "I don't think there's been anything wrong with the people they've sent."

"They weren't you." At this confession my head swings around, and he shrugs, "I like working with you, Crazy. It makes the days a little bit easier."

I feel my face soften, and a million questions rattle around in my head, but I settle on the one that has me the most curious. "If money wasn't a consideration, what would you have done?"

"I would have been a social worker." His answer is immediate. He takes hold of my hand, and starts teasing his thumb around in soft circles as he continues. "When I was a teenager I used to go to this after-school program that was run by a non-profit. The guy that ran it, Michael, was awesome. He kept us on the straight and narrow, and gave us the guidance that we didn't always get at home." Concentrating on our hands, he continues his gentle touch. "But it was more than that. He actually cared about us. He helped me find a program that donated sports equipment to students in need, so I could play football. When I was struggling in History, he found a volunteer tutor for me. He just made life that little bit easier. It would've been cool to pay it forward, and do that for someone." Shaking off the seriousness, he leans over and places a kiss behind my ear, causing me to shiver. "I make sure I donate money to a bunch of programs so I don't feel like a complete asshole."

"You know it's not too lat—" my words are cut off

as we hit some turbulence and my hands latch onto the armrests so tight that my knuckles turn white.

Mason chuckles at my reaction.

"Is my girl scared of flying? I didn't think you were scared of anything."

"I'm not," I hiss. He laughs, and I swear to my god, Channing Tatum, that if my hands weren't glued to these armrests, he'd be getting a purple nurple right about now. Because sometimes no matter how old you are, a purple nurple is the answer.

"How about I distract you?" Mason nuzzles into me, and his teeth nip at my earlobe which sends a direct jolt of pleasure to my clit. "How about I tell you everything I have planned for you when we get home?"

"That might work. It would have to be pretty good though. You think you're up to the challenge, Sunshine?"

A wicked smile is his only response.

Mason throws the door to his apartment open and motions for me to enter. As he follows me through he pushes the door shut with one hand, and grabs me around the waist with the other, swinging me around and pushing me up against the wall.

His hands cup my face, and his mouth lands on mine while his hips jerk forward, pushing his already hard cock into my pussy. I failed to put on panties this morning, and I can already feel my arousal dripping down my thighs. After spending a five-hour flight listening to all the filthy things he had planned for me, I could almost come from this alone.

"I can feel you, Crazy, you're so fucking wet, I can practically smell it." He thrusts up, causing me to gasp.

"Fuuuuck. Do that again," I demand.

He grinds against me again, dragging his hands down my body until they find the hem of my Maxi dress, and pulls it up until it's bunched around my waist.

His tongue wrestles with mine fiercely; but as he slides a hand down, seeking the heat of my pussy, he slows our kiss until the intensity of his mouth, combined with the sensation of his fingers trailing along my skin, cause my head to spin and goosebumps to break out.

When his fingers find my bare cunt, he stills for a moment, pulling his head back and smirking down at me.

Then in a movement that makes my heart stutter, he roughly picks me up and heads further into the apartment.

I'm oblivious to where we're going, my mouth is on his neck, and my tongue is tracing a delicious pattern, enjoying the taste of him.

I'm suddenly thrown down effortlessly, landing on a cloud that I quickly realize is his bed.

Mason is on me before I even realize what's going on. My dress gets pushed back up and his hands are splayed on my thighs, opening me up for him.

He looks up and holds my eye as he lowers his head. His hot breath causes my pussy to pulse and just before

I feel his tongue leisurely lick along my slit, he winks at me.

Before I can respond to that dick move, the heat of his tongue forces a loud moan from me, and my hands quickly tangle in his hair.

Pulling away, he thrusts two fingers in me and starts moving them slowly.

"You taste fucking amazing, baby. I might just spend the next few hours eating you out. You want that?" His lips close around my clit, and he sucks it roughly before using his tongue to circle it quickly, with the perfect amount of pressure. I'm desperate to come already, and my hands push down harder on his head.

He removes his fingers, and I let out a hiss at the loss of sensation, but they are quickly replaced with his tongue and as he thrusts it in and out, his thumb finds my clit and rolls over it, creating the perfect riot of sensations. I feel my orgasm building and start to roll my pelvis, riding his face as best I can from this position.

"Oh god, fuck me Mason, oh my fucking god, don't stop. Pleasepleasepleaseplease, don't stop."

His tongue and thumb both pick up speed and in a matter of minutes I am coming spectacularly, screaming out my release.

Mason slows his movements as my body goes limp, and my hands loosen their grip on his hair. When the tremors of my body subside, he places a final kiss on my clit before lifting his head and moving up along my body. Our mouths clash, and when he sucks my tongue into his mouth I taste myself on him. It's fucking delicious.

He kisses along my jaw and down my neck until he reaches my collarbone, and tattoo. Using his tongue, he traces along the script, *I was not built to break*, before softly kissing it.

"I think tongue fucking you just might be my favorite thing ever," he whispers, drawing a low laugh from me.

"I hope you don't think you're finished? You made all kinds of promises that I'm expecting you to keep."

"Get that fucking dress off now," he growls.

I hurriedly sit up and pull my dress up over my torso, revealing my bare breasts. His eyes widen at the sight, and his hand goes straight to his cock which is still confined in denim.

"You have got to be fucking kidding me, Crazy." His voice is pained. "You have pierced tits?" And then like a heat-seeking missile his mouth latches onto one breast, his teeth gently tugging on the barbell, while his hand finds the other, and pulls.

I fall back, overwhelmed with pleasure, and Mason is quick to continue his assault on my tits. His hands are everywhere, somehow both rough and gentle, while he uses my piercings to keep me right on the verge of coming again.

Ripping his mouth away from me, he looks at me from under his lashes. "You have the Goldilocks of tits, baby, you have no idea."

I pick this moment to giggle for the first time in my life. "Goldilocks, huh?"

"Yep, not too big, not too small." A lazy grin crosses his beautiful face. "Just right. And fucking pierced. You're killing me, you know that, right?" He reaches down and twists one of my nipples, causing my breath to hitch. "I'm going to have to fuck these tits one day."

My hand reaches out, stroking up his inked arm, teasing him with my fingernails. "What's wrong with today?"

Leaning away, he looks at me, trying to gauge my sincerity, but I know that he'll see nothing but desire in my eyes.

"Abso-fucking-lutely nothing." He stands up, and reaching behind him yanks his t-shirt over his head before moving his hands to his zipper while at the same time toeing his shoes off. Everything seems to move in slow motion as I watch his fingers drag the zip down, holding my breath as I wait to get my first glimpse of the cock that gave me the best orgasm I had ever experienced. At least until about five minutes ago, that is. A magic cock *and* a magic tongue, it would seem I hit the jackpot with Mason Alexander.

His hands move to his hips and slowly drag the jeans down revealing a mouth-watering V that leads to a shaft that, while not even fully exposed, has my eyes widening.

When he finishes removing his pants, it's all I can do to stop myself from jumping up and doing a happy dance. Long. Thick. Hard, and pointing straight at me, it looks like Mason has the Goldilocks of dicks. Fuck yeah, Skye is going to hear about this!

He reaches down, and a gasp escapes me as he drags

three fingers through my pussy, before using my cum to lube himself up. "You get so fucking wet for me, Crazy, I love it." Lowering himself down, he starts placing open-mouthed kisses between my breasts, his tongue tasting me, leaving a trail of wet, exposed skin.

Moving up along my body until he is straddling my chest, Mason leans down to lay a kiss on me that makes every single one of my pulse points race.

Straightening up, he caresses my breasts before taking hold of his cock and teasing the tip over my nipples, eliciting a loud moan. Placing himself between my tits, he pushes them together, creating a snug little hideaway.

"Put your hands here, and keep them pushed together. I need to fuck these tits now." His voice is gravelly and rough, and he's having trouble getting the words out.

We move in perfect rhythm, as if we've done this a million times before. Mason starts with slow, shallow thrusts, and every time his dick peeks out through the tunnel of my breasts I can't help but stick out my tongue and swipe it across the tip. He starts to pick up speed and grabs hold of the bedhead to anchor himself. I have to hold tight to keep my breasts in place while he thrusts harder and faster.

The low rasping moans he's making are creating an intense throb in my clit, and the visual of him above me, and his cock sliding along my chest has my eyes rolling back in pleasure.

Letting out a loud grunt, he pulls away and takes

himself in hand, jerking off until he climaxes loudly, his cum shooting out over my breasts.

Taking a moment to catch his breath, he sits back on his heels, and his eyes roam all over my body, until they settle on my breasts.

"Well, would you look at that," his tone is undeniably mischievous. "You've been frosted by Mason."

❧

That night we are seated at Mason's small dining table, naked and eating Chinese takeout from the containers while we laugh over embarrassing childhood stories.

"You know your apartment isn't at all what I expected." Mason turns and looks around his small apartment, and my eyes follow. It's a small two-bedroom apartment, with an open plan that features a living area and a compact eat-in kitchen. A far cry from the extravagant penthouse I figured he would live in.

"I mean, don't get me wrong, it's beautiful." And it was. With solid timber floorboards in a gorgeous dark oak, walls painted a soft gray and large picture windows, the overwhelming feeling was one of warmth and welcome.

"There's only me, anything bigger seemed excessive. Just because I have money doesn't mean I have to waste it." Pushing away from the table, he's standing in front of the fridge in two easy strides. "You want another water?" It takes me a second to answer because I'm trying to stop myself from getting up and biting his delectable ass.

I shake my head to clear the image, and am just about to answer when his cell phone rings next to me on the table. It's his personal ringtone, so throwing him a cheeky grin, I snatch up the phone and answer.

"Good evening, you've reached Mason and his colossal cock, how may I be of assistance?"

"Fuck, Crazy!" Mason races over and attempts to grab the phone, but I'm too quick, and run around to the other side of the table to escape him.

There's silence on the line, and I'm about to hang up when I hear a voice that makes my heart drop. "Cassidy?"

Oh. Fuck.

"Rhonda! Hi! Oh my god, I'm so sorry, I was just messing around. I haven't seen his cock, I swear." I look up and Mason is watching me with a look of curious horror, and I want the ground to open up and swallow me.

"Well, that's a damn shame, Cassidy. My son could do with a girl like you in his life."

"Really?" My voice is hesitant. That's not the response I was expecting, after my foot-in-mouth hello.

"Really, Cassidy. He needs some fun in his life and you, sweetheart, are probably the perfect one to make that happen." My hand tightens around the phone, and I start nibbling on my bottom lip. I have no idea why Rhonda's approval means so much, but from the swell of emotion I'm feeling, it does.

Turning my back on Mason, I reply, "Thank you, Rhonda. That means a lot."

"Okay, well, I will let you get back to whatever it is you weren't doing, and we'll talk later."

"You didn't want to talk to Mason?"

"No, it wasn't anything important. I'll catch him another time. You take care, okay?"

"I will. You too, bye."

After taking a second to compose myself, I turn and face Mason.

"You alright over there?" His eyes are warm, and I smile brightly at him.

"Yep, but you've worn me out, Sunshine. I think it's time for me to head home."

He comes over to stand in front of me, pushing his body flush with mine and tweaking a nipple, straddling the line of pleasure and pain before leaning down and placing a soft kiss on the tip of my nose.

"You don't have to go. Stay the night."

"Are you sure?"

"Definitely. I even promise to let you get some sleep. I have some more work to do, anyway."

He takes hold of my hand and pulls me toward his bedroom. Once we're all settled I look over at him, sitting up in bed with his laptop balanced on his knees, and an array of papers spread out beside him.

"This account seems really complicated, are they all this difficult?"

"Fuck no. And there's no reason that this one should be either, except that Alistair Thompson is the biggest asshole you will ever come across, and keeps moving the goalposts. Every time we make an offer, he agrees subject to minor changes, which then turn into major changes, and we have to re-work the entire proposal. We were this close to getting a contract signed about a month ago, when he suddenly decided he had an issue with one of the clauses. He's a total fuckwit."

"Wait a minute!" I sit up, pulling the sheet with me and cross my legs. "Did you say *Alistair* Thompson?"

"Yeah, why?"

"Shortish guy, early sixties, kind of handsome in a distinguished old guy way?"

"Jesus, Cass, I don't know. I guess so."

"I know him! He used to live down the street from us when I was a kid. I actually think my mom still keeps in touch with his wife." I shudder as I start to recall all the stories I heard about him over the years. "Ugh, you're right though, he's the biggest dickhole! He used to cheat on his wife all the time. Everyone except his wife and kids knew about it. I used to feel so bad for them."

Mason's eyes narrow at my news, turning calculating. I recognize that look from work, and for a brief moment I worry that I shouldn't have shared this information with him. But just as quickly as it came, the look vanishes.

"I can't say anything about that man surprises me." The disgust is evident in his voice.

"Yep, total douche canoe. How much work do you have?" I ask, changing the subject.

"A couple of hours." Leaning over, he wraps my hair

around his fist and pulls me toward him, his mouth covering mine and his tongue licking along my bottom lip before he pulls away. "Get some sleep while you can. You never know, I may wake you up for a midnight snack later." And as I roll over and attempt to sleep, I clench my thighs at the promise his voice held.

CHAPTER TEN

MASON

"Right, that sounds good, add the addendum to the current contract, and hopefully that will finally please the fucker." Samuels' laugh on the other end of the line is hollow.

"One can only hope. Alright, I'll get that drawn up now and couriered straight over to him. Enjoy your day off, man, you deserve it."

"Thanks. I'll see you tomorrow, but if anything urgent comes up I have my cell on me." With no further preamble I hang up the phone, and make my way to the elevator in Cassidy's building.

As I wait impatiently for it to arrive, my mind wanders back to last weekend. She threw me for a fucking loop telling me she knew Thompson, and spilling that juicy little titbit about him. I have to admit, it crossed my mind for a brief moment that I might be able to use that information to compel him to sign the contracts. Put this motherfucker of an account to bed once and for all.

Just as quickly, I realized that blackmail is illegal, and I wasn't prepared to risk my freedom for a job I wasn't even sure I wanted anymore.

The lift arrives, and as the doors open I stalk inside, quickly pressing the button for the fourth floor. I scrub my hands across my face in an effort to push thoughts of work from my mind.

Ever since my talk with Cassidy I have been questioning my commitment to my job even more intensely. She's right. It doesn't matter how much money I make, my mother is never going to allow me to take care of her. So why am I doing this? Why the hell am I working ninety hours a week, busting my ass doing a job I hate?

I am quickly thrust back to reality when the doors open, and Cassidy is standing right in front of me, purse in hand. As I walk toward her, her expression morphs from shock to happiness to suspicion in a mere nanosecond, and I take a moment to appreciate how fucking beautiful it is that she never tries to hide herself from me.

"What are you doing here, Sunshine? I'm not coming into work, not even if you try and use your powers of dicksuasion on me."

"Jesus, what the hell is dicksuasion? You do realize that you can't just go around inventing words, right?"

"Dicksuasion. The act of convincing me to do something by using your magnificent, giant cock. Dicksuasion." She waggles her eyebrows at me, and I wrap my arm around her waist, pulling her close.

"Magnificent, giant cock, huh?" My lips find the

spot behind her ear that makes her sigh in that way I like.

"Uh huh." She leans into me, her hand fisting my t-shirt. "Skye was very impressed." My tongue stops the path it was tracing. Did she say Skye?

Pulling away, I'm met with angelic Cassidy, all wide eyed and shit.

"You told Skye abou— You know what? I don't want to know. C'mon, let's go." I take hold of her hand and spin us around, pressing the button to get the elevator back up.

"Wait, where are we going? Why aren't you at work? What is this madness?" She steps back and looks me up and down, taking in my jeans and t-shirt, her eyes linger on my junk, and I fight back a smirk.

"Hey, my eyes are up here, Crazy. I'm not a piece of meat you know."

"You're not dressed for work, I see." Her eyes widen. "Are you playing hooky, Sunshine? Oh my god, please tell me I'm popping your hooky cherry, please for the love of Channing Tatum!" Cassidy is literally bouncing in front of me. This is definitely not the first time I've played hooky, but who am I to burst her bubble?

"Yep, I would only do this for you, baby." My mouth lands on hers, and I slide my tongue along her bottom lip before entering and tasting her. Too soon, we are distracted by the arrival of the elevator, and I take hold of her hand, turning to pull her into it, just as she turns and starts trying to pull me in the opposite direction.

"Whoa, what are you doing? We're going this way."

We're playing tug of war, each trying to pull the other to their side.

"Why would we leave the building? It's Friday and you're not working. We have three days; think of all the sexcapades we can have!" I pause, because fuck, she makes a compelling argument. But no, I have a plan and best boyfriend status to secure.

"Nope." I take off into the elevator, pulling her behind me. "Trust me, you'll be glad you came."

"Aw, Sunshine, I'm always glad to come. But Princess is pissed, fair warning."

"Who the hell is Princess?" I question, baffled.

"Ugh, it doesn't matter, she doesn't want to talk to you right now, anyway." Cassidy sighs dramatically, before crossing her arms over her chest, pushing those incredible tits out, and pouting.

"Where are we going anyway?" she grumbles. "Am I dressed okay?"

I look over at her, for the first time taking the time to note what she's wearing. Her long legs are encased in black leggings that are essentially a second skin, and she's wearing this white t-shirt thing that hangs off one shoulder. My fingers itch to touch the exposed skin. Her pink hair is piled up on top of her head in a messy bun, and black flip flops complete the outfit.

"You look perfect, Crazy." As the doors open we step out into the lobby of her apartment building. "Where were you headed, anyway?"

"Starbucks. A venti iced caramel cocoa cluster frappuccino was calling my name.

"Jesus, that's a mouthful. But then you're dating

me, so I guess you're used to a mouthful." As we step out onto the pavement, I turn to give her a smirk but when I'm met with a downcast Cassidy, chewing on her bottom lip, I stop in my tracks. "I can see your brain ticking, Cassidy, what's going on?"

"Is that what we're doing? Dating?" That's what she's worried about?

"You said give it a go, Crazy, so fuck yeah we're dating. I'm all in here." I pull her into an embrace, oblivious to the people rushing by us. It takes her a second, but she wraps her arms around my waist and places a soft kiss on my jaw.

"Me too."

"Alright, if we're done with the emotional BS, we need to grab a cab. Let's go."

Moments later we're situated in a taxi, headed toward the upper west side. Checking my watch, I see that we're right on schedule. I can't wait to see her face when we arrive.

Forty-five minutes of endless questions later, we come to a stop on Columbus Avenue in front of the iconic *Magnolia Bakery*.

I'm still paying the driver when Cassidy begins pushing past me in an effort to get out, and I'm left with a face full of ass. Hers is pretty spectacular though, so I'm not complaining. Instead, I give it a slap and push her out onto the sidewalk, following close behind.

"I don't know whether to kiss you or punch you right now, Sunshine. This is my favorite bakery, but if you wanted a cupcake, I'm kind of pissed you didn't ask me. I make a pretty damn good one, you know."

"Don't be like that, I love your cupcakes, babe." She rolls her eyes at me as I move us over by the entrance, out of the way of the bustling crowd.

"So, I know how much you love frosting," I can't help giving her a little wink, but when she looks ready to slap me, I rush on, "I remembered you said you wanted to learn some new icing techniques and it was something you were looking into. Then I remembered Tanya telling me something about being dragged to a class here for some bridal shower. So, I checked it out and booked us in for a class today."

Cassidy stares at me, eyes wide, lips slightly parted, as if she's not quite sure what I'm saying. Then her face splits into a huge grin, and she throws herself into my arms.

"Best. Boyfriend. Ever! I'll totally let you frost me tonight, big boy!" Grabbing my hand, she drags me inside, and the weirdest thing? There's nowhere I'd rather be.

Two hours later I'm walking out the same door, with a box of cupcakes in hand, and a babbling girlfriend by my side. Cassidy was in her element in there, hanging on every word the instructor spoke. Watching her work her magic was incredible. She was focused and methodical, and I had to stifle a laugh at one point as I realized what a contrast it was to her work ethic in the office. But it also made it glaringly obvious that an office is not where she belongs. This is her passion. It's what she needs to be doing, and I'll do whatever I can to make sure that happens.

"How amazing was that Lambeth Method piping technique? Ugh, I have to practice that this weekend." Turning around so she is walking backward and facing me, oblivious to the people scattering to avoid her, she takes my hand. "Thank you for that, it was incredible. And I have never seen anything funnier than you attempting to decorate a cupcake. It was fucking hilarious."

"That's because I'm used to dealing with extra-big equipment." And just to make sure she doesn't miss my meaning I adjust myself and throw her a wink.

"Whatever." Rolling her eyes, she turns around, and takes hold of my arm. "Oh, thank fuck, there's a coffee shop. I need to run in and grab some caffeine." As Cassidy starts making her way in that direction, my eyes are drawn back to a shopfront we just passed.

"You go in, I just need to run an errand. Can you grab me a coffee, and I'll meet you there in five?"

"Yeah, sure. Don't take too long, though, I want to get home and start baking."

"Five minutes, Crazy. Learn some patience, babe." Her eyes narrow into a glare, but she remains silent as she walks into the shop. Hauling ass, I turn around and make my way back in the direction we just came. Entering the little store, I head straight to the girl behind the counter. In just minutes I'm holding the handcrafted necklace I spotted in the window. It's a small brushed silver disc with the image of a tiny dandelion with seeds blowing away, and the phrase *"never stop making wishes"* engraved on it. It's both whimsical and hopeful, and reminded me of Cassidy immediately.

After impatiently waiting for the necklace to be wrapped, I pay and then take my time on the walk back, enjoying the sense of freedom. I need more days like this in my life.

I walk through the door to the coffee shop exactly five minutes later, and spot my girl immediately. Sitting at a table by the window, she is lost in herself, staring unseeingly at the crowd outside, twirling a strand of hair that's fallen free, around a finger. She's oblivious to my approach, and when I bend down and place a kiss on the curve of her neck, allowing my tongue to sneak out for a taste, she startles, whipping her head around with venom in her eyes.

"Whoa, easy there, tiger. It's just me."

"That's a good way to get a face full of mace, Sunshine." Her hand reaches up to stroke my cheek. "I would hate to hurt all that pretty." She punctuates this with a gentle slap to the cheek.

"Smartass. I guess you don't want the present I just got you." I shrug. "Your loss." I start to move away, but her response is immediate.

"Wait! I want a present! What'd you get me?" A huge grin is plastered across her face, and with a flourish I present her with the small gift wrapped in tissue paper. Cassidy squeals in delight, grabbing it from my hands and ripping the paper off.

When she has uncovered the necklace she stares at it, unblinking. I wait for the excitement, but instead her face drops, and her eyes glisten with tears. Using a finger, she lightly traces the image of the dandelion before she looks up at me, her face awash with anguish.

"I need to go." With that, she gets up and makes her way out onto the street, leaving me standing there wondering what the hell just happened.

CHAPTER ELEVEN

*K*eep it together, Jensen. Keep it fucking together.

My hand is on the door of the taxi when he catches up with me. He slides onto the seat right beside me, and I can feel his confusion just as clearly as I can feel my own. Today, for the first time, I wasn't comparing him to a ghost. To a memory. Today, I was in the moment, and it felt fucking fantastic.

Then he had to go and ruin it with that mother-fucking necklace. And I can't even be pissed at him. The expression on his face when he offered me that gift was enough to heal my broken heart. Before shattering it all over again.

The only words spoken throughout the drive is my address, and my body is wound tight. I spend the entire ride with my forehead pressed against the window, playing with a lock of hair and watching the world speed past in a blur.

Memories are crowding my mind, a highlight reel

of my time with Aidan playing on a loop, creating a tightness in my chest.

I've spent the last nine years searching for that connection I felt with him. So why, when I've finally found it, do I feel as though I'm betraying him?

Finally, my apartment building appears up ahead and I feel my shoulders sag in relief, knowing the comfort of my home is within reach.

Minutes later we are making our way inside when his hand takes mine, and I glance down to see our fingers laced together. A warmth runs through my body and I feel my fingers instinctively squeeze, attempting to offer him some comfort as regret seeps into my consciousness.

Fuck. I'm a complete cuntmuffin. And I have some explaining to do.

My hand shakes slightly as I unlock the door and as we enter, the familiar scent of vanilla sweetness hits me, and strong arms wrap me up tight.

"Talk, Crazy." His voice is low, and his breath tickles my ear, causing a tingle to travel down my spine. "If you're going to live up to your nickname, I at least want to know what I did."

I turn in his arms, looking up into those hazel eyes that hold nothing but concern right now. "I'm sorry."

My breath catches as my legs are yanked up, and I'm in Mason's arms as he carries me across the room, dropping my ass on the kitchen counter.

"Don't be sorry. Just tell me what happened."

"Ugh, Jesus, I had a meltdown, okay? If I told you I was experiencing my own personal *Red Wedding* would you let it slide?" His face squints in confusion, before realization dawns and it morphs into a look of disgust.

"*That* is a fucking nasty euphemism, Cass. And no, I wouldn't. So start talking."

Taking a deep breath, I prepare to expose myself to him. And not in the fun way. "Dandelions were my favorite flowers. Behind my parent's house there is this little park, and it's full of wildflowers. I always loved the dandelions best, because they were my favorite color, but also because they didn't die like all of the other flowers. Instead they turned into wish fairies." Mason quirks an eyebrow. "Hey, don't judge, I was a kid! I don't know how many hours I spent wishing on those damn weeds. But I swear there were times it worked. That's how I got my baby sister, you know."

His forehead meets mine. "Is that so?"

"Yep, Layla owes her life to me. Although she's not nearly grateful enough if you ask me." His laugh echoes throughout the room.

"Okay, I'm with you so far. But I'm still not under-standing why me giving you the necklace, made you sad."

"I was on the phone to Aidan when his car crashed. He had called me to tell me he had left something for me. The sounds of the car—" I cut myself off as my throat closes up and tears threaten. The voices of those boys still haunt me. The fear and anguish; I heard it all. And there are moments still, when I am crushed under the weight of my own fear, the memory of their cries mingle with mine and I struggle to breathe.

"Baby." Hands tangle in my hair, the sensation

bringing me back to the present. "I can't even imagine what that was like, I'm so sorry." I lift my head slightly until my lips are almost touching his.

"He had left me dandelions. That's why he had called." His eyes close briefly at this, before opening and meeting mine.

"I'm sorry I made you sad, baby."

"You make me a lot of things, Mason. There are times I want to love you, times I want to murder you, and then there are times I want to fuck your brains out. But you have never once made me sad." Kissing his nose, I add, "Believe dat."

"Believe *dat*?"

"*Believe* dat."

His mouth quirks up before meeting mine in a searing kiss, his lips soft as they move against mine. The combination of his cologne, and the taste of sweetness that still lingers on his tongue, overwhelms me in a heady rush of sensations.

There's an urgency in our touch, his hands still fisted in my hair, pulling me closer in an attempt to deepen our kiss while my hands roam over his broad chest.

Breaking away, Mason eyes me with lewd intent in his eye, sending my girlie bits all aflutter.

Then in a flash we are a frenzy of movement, clothes being tossed carelessly. I maneuver my leggings and panties down, while Mason works his zipper down, and pulls his cock free.

I watch his hand as he strokes himself roughly, my

eyes drawn to the muscles twitching in his forearm, and the effect it has on his tattoos.

"You planning on finishing the job yourself, Sunshine, because this is quite a show."

"Baby, I am going to fuck you now, but if you don't watch that smart mouth of yours, I'll fuck that instead of your pussy. You want that?" The wetness I can feel coat my thighs makes it pretty fucking clear that Princess would be mighty miffed if I blew her chance of riding the d-train right now, so I keep my mouth shut.

Stepping into me, he thrusts forward forcefully, pounding into me in the most heart stopping way.

Arching up, my mouth clashes with his as my hand slides over his ass, pulling him closer. I can never seem to get close enough.

His hands have settled on my hips, and he pulls me toward him, meeting him thrust for thrust. The sound of our bodies slamming into each other is almost enough to tip me over the edge, and when Mason's fingers close around my nipple, tweaking the barbell there, and his raspy voice whispers, "Scream for me, Crazy." I do just that.

"You seem happy, CJ." The cutlery clatters as we set the table, and I meet my baby sister's eyes across the table.

"Thanks, bub, I am. I think I might have actually met my match. He definitely keeps me on my toes." My nose scrunches in good humor, and Layla giggles.

"How long has it been now?"

"Officially? A month, but it feels like longer."

"I like seeing you like this. I've missed it." Her voice is soft, and I pull her in for a tight hug.

"What about you, Lay? Is everything working itself out with the Ethan situation? You know I'll kick his ass for you, right? I don't care how long I've known him." I feel my shackles rise at the idea of someone hurting her. She has the sweetest heart of anyone I know.

"I don't want to talk about it. Please?"

"Cassidy!" My mom's voice interrupts us, so I give Layla a reprieve.

"What?"

Mom enters the room, tucking a strand of pale blonde hair behind her ear. "There's no need to yell, sweet thing. Make us a jug of margaritas, please. Layla, your father needs some help at the grill, but he refuses to let me near it. Can you give him a hand, love?"

"Sure thing, Mom."

"I'm just going to run to the shops, your father needs beer apparently." She rolls her eyes in mock frustration and I laugh as she grabs her purse, and leaves me alone.

Ten minutes later I'm finishing up the cocktails when my phone rings and a picture of Mason's delicious ding-a-ling lights up my screen. Yeah, he's going to kill me when he finds out about that.

"Wassup, buttercup?"

"Hey, Crazy, how's your day going?"

"Fan-fucking-tastic. I'm about to start day drinking,

which is obvs one of my favorite things. What time do you think you'll get here?"

"Baby." I can already tell from his tone that I'm not going to like what comes next. "I'm sorry, but the company's lawyer has asked for an emergency meeting about this Thompson shitshow. I'm not going to be able to make it."

"Oh." The disappointment is like a punch to the gut, but I know this can't be helped. Mason wouldn't bail unless he had no choice. "That's okay. But I thought everything had been finalized with that account?"

I hear his sigh through the phone line, and I can just imagine him leaning back in his desk chair, running a hand through his hair in frustration.

"So did I. The last we heard we were given the go ahead, and everything was supposed to be moving forward. But, apparently, he has some fucking issue with the wording. So, Stella and I are going to try and salvage it."

"Stella? Is that *the* Stella, Sunshine? Should I be worried?"

"You have nothing to worry about, baby." There's a pause and then I can hear a muffled voice in the background. "Cass, I have to go. Can you let your parents know how sorry I am?"

"Of course, don't worry about it, babe, they'll understand."

"I love you, Crazy. I'll come to yours when I'm done, okay?"

"Don't be too late, or I'll trade your cock in for my

BOB, 'kay? I love you, bye-eee!" And I hang up on him before he can respond.

Wait what did I just say to him?

"Do I even wanna know?" I spin around and come face to face with Layla.

"Uh, no probably not," I reply, shrugging, and doing my best to shake off the shock I feel. "Mason can't make it. Work shit came up." Her face drops, but she recovers quickly.

"Bummer, but these things happen when you're dating an important businessman, I guess."

"Oh my god, do not call him that to his face, his ego doesn't need any extra inflation. Now, let's get our day drink on!"

Hours later I am making my way up to the seventy-fourth floor offices with a red velvet cupcake in my hand and thoughts of desk sex on my mind.

The offices are quiet tonight, which is unusual. Annoying workaholics can normally be found working around the clock. And yes, I am including my boyfriend in that group.

Turning the corner, I have only made it a few feet when a woman I assume is Stella, exits Mason's office, adjusting her bra. Looking up she catches my eye, and I swear I see a flicker of a smile cross her face, but it's gone before I can be sure.

Walking toward her I take in her petite frame. Her long chestnut hair falls straight down her back, looking sleek and stylish, while the LBD she's wearing straddles the line of business-like and sexy. She walks with an alluring sway to her hips, and the confidence of a woman who knows exactly how beautiful she is.

The sound of a cell phone ringing fills the air, and Stella pulls out her phone, answering it in an abrupt tone. Her voice is strong, and loud enough that I can hear her, even though she is still a distance away.

"Tre, I want you to schedule a conference call with Thompson tomorrow, I think I've figured out how to deal with the asshole once and for all. And Mason is emailing through a doc that I'll need on my desk first thing." She pauses briefly, listening to the voice on the other end of the line, and then laughs quietly. "Absolutely. Bouncing on that man's dick is enough to cheer anyone up." She is right in front of me when these words fall out of her stupid, pouty mouth. And then the bitch winks at me. Fucking. Winks.

She obviously has no idea who I am, because her steps don't falter, and she continues down the corridor without a look back, while I stand there stupefied.

I watch her until she disappears from view, and then coming to my senses, I turn on my heel and storm toward what tomorrow will be known as the site of Mason Alexander's death.

Bursting through the door, I don't even bother trying to control my level of pissed off. "Did you fuck that sluttinator, Sunshine? Do I need to cut your dick off? Because I'll do it, fuckmunch, don't doubt that for a second."

Mason looks up from his desk, where he's hunched over a pile of documents, with a look of confusion.

"What the fuck are you talking about?"

"Did. You. Fuck. The. Lawyer." I hiss out each word.

"Stella? No, of course not. Why the hell would you even ask that?"

"Because she was just on the phone bragging about bouncing on your dick, that's why, asswipe."

He pushes away from his desk, and storms over to me, forcing me backward until I hit the wall where he pins me with his hips and cages me between his arms.

"Enough. I did not fuck Stella. Look around, Crazy. Does this room look like anyone just had sex in here?" He leans down and brushes his nose along my neck. "Does it smell like someone just had sex in here?"

Looking around, I have to admit he has a point.

"Eyes on me." His voice is demanding, challenging me. "I am not a cheater, Cassidy. Don't ever question that."

My body slumps as the adrenaline leaves my body, but he catches me. Metaphorically, as well as literally.

"I told her about us tonight. Not who you are, obviously, but that I was involved with someone. She was pissed. Of course. I'm a fucking good lay." He places a kiss on the tip of my nose, and I giggle. When the hell did I become a giggler? I want to bitch slap myself so bad right now.

"I don't know why she said what she said, but you have to know that you never need to worry about that. I'll do plenty of things that you'll want to kill me for, but fucking around isn't one of them. Understood?"

"Understood." The air is thick with tension, my chest is tight, and when he lays his forehead against mine, I blurt out, "I said I love you."

"You did." His voice is matter of fact, and I have no clue what he's thinking.

"I was joking." My voice is barely a whisper.

"Crazy?"

"Yeah?"

"I love you." His lips meet mine briefly. "And I'm not joking."

A breath that I didn't realize I was holding, rushes out of me, and I'm ready to jump him when his voice interrupts me.

"Was that for me?" My eyes follow his and I spot the cupcake where it must have fallen during my dramatic entrance.

"Yep." The look of devastation on his face is priceless, and I have to fight a laugh. "I have more at home. Are you done here?"

Looking back at his desk, he shrugs. "Yeah, I can do the rest at home. Just give me a sec, and I'll be ready."

"Did your meeting go well, then? Non-sexually speaking, that is."

He throws a glare my way before responding. "Actually, yeah. I'm pretty sure we won't have any more trouble from Thompson, thank God."

He's gathering up the paperwork when his phone starts vibrating. Answering, he puts it on speakerphone and barks out, "What do you want, dickface?"

Ben's booming laugh fills the air. "Dude, you've been hanging around Cassidy too long." I roll my eyes and make a gagging motion, watching as Mason tries to suppress a laugh.

"I'm about to head home, BJ." My eyes widen until I'm scared they're going to pop out of my head. *BJ?* I. am. dying. "What do you need?"

"It's Jack's birthday next week, so we're going out drinking. Are you in?"

"Spanky!" I lose the battle to keep my mouth shut. "Or is it BJ? Maybe I should just call you Blowie? Dick muncher? There's just so many wonderful choices!"

My outburst is met with stony silence.

"Mason, you're dead to me, you fucker. Dead!"

"Aw, don't be like that, Blowie, *I* love *you*!"

"You're an evil she-devil, Cassidy Jensen. And stop asking Skye about my dick, it's fucking weird. Mason, see you next week. Eight o'clock at The Irish Pub on 7th Avenue." And with that he's gone.

"Why the hell are you asking about his dick?" Mason's tone of righteous indignation tickles my funny bone.

"Well, looky here. Seems I'm not the only one who gets jealous, hey?"

"No, seriously. Why are you asking about my best friend's dick, Crazy?"

"Ugh, because it embarrasses her, and skeeves him out. Win win. Happy?" Honestly, he looks far from it. He has that cute little frown line across his brow going on, and his full mouth is pursed slightly, just begging me to lick it into submission.

"I'm tired, Sunshine. Take me home." And as he

takes my hand, and leads me out the door, a thought occurs to me.

"How pissed would Spanky be if I crashed your boys' night? He would love it, right?" I clap my hands with evil glee. "Ooooh, we're gonna have so much fun!"

CHAPTER TWELVE

MASON

"Jesus, check them out." Ben slaps a hand on my shoulder as he takes a seat on the stool next to me.

I move my focus to our friends, who are lined up at the bar, downing shots.

"Right? My head is pounding just at the thought of the amount of alcohol they're putting away." Christ, when did I get so old?

I point to the light beer he's lifting to his mouth. "You're sticking to the light stuff?"

Ben smirks at me over the lip of the bottle. "I've got a beautiful woman waiting for me at home, whiskey dick is not part of my plans tonight."

The tumbler of whiskey making its way to my mouth stops in its track.

"Asshole." I place the glass back down on the bar.

"Hey, you should be thanking me. Could you imagine the shit Cassidy would give you if you couldn't get it up?" He cringes. "She'd crucify you."

A loud laugh escapes me as I imagine her reaction.

"Fuck, she'd probably pull out her vibrator and finish herself off right in front of me. My girl likes her orgasms too much to go without."

Ben groans next to me. "I don't need to know that, dude."

We fall into an easy silence, both lost in our own world despite the chaotic atmosphere around us. The loud voices and laughter combine with the music being played to create a wave of sound that vibrates through my body.

My mind is filled with Cassidy, and that scares the fuck out of me. One month. One month is all it's taken for her to wiggle that ass of hers into every facet of my life. One month is all it took for me to tell her that I love her. How many months will it take for me to get over her, when she decides that what I have to offer will never be enough?

Motioning the bartender over, I follow Ben's lead and order a beer. Once I have the bottle in my hand I get his attention and point to the door. "Fresh air?" Ben nods in agreement, and we push our way through the bodies packed tightly into the bar, until we practically fall out onto the street.

"So, I know I gave up on this years ago, but a pretty little bird told me that you've started taking Sundays off. You wanna come and watch the game this weekend?"

"A pretty little bird, huh?" I give a slight shake of my head and chuckle. "Is there anything those girls don't tell each other?"

"Trust me, you don't want to know the answer to that."

Taking a long pull of my beer, the slight bitterness rolls around in my mouth.

"Is it weird that I feel like this could be it?" My question is random, but Ben doesn't even hesitate, understanding immediately what I'm saying.

"No. I knew after one night with Skye. It wasn't anything tangible that I can explain, but I knew. And even when I thought I didn't know, *I knew*."

The humor leaves his face at the memory of his monumental fuck up that almost caused him to lose Skye.

"You were a huge asshole. You didn't deserve to get her back, you realize that, right?"

"Yeah, I know." He looks pained, and I know without a shadow of a doubt that even though Skye has forgiven him, it'll be a long time before he forgives himself.

"So, how are things going with Cassidy?" His mouth spreads in a huge grin. "You know, when Skye told me, I thought she was bullshitting. Cassidy is definitely not who I saw you with."

"Man, I wanted to kill her for the first six weeks." Scratching my jaw, I consider what I just said. "Hell, there are moments I still want to kill her. But it's like my entire fucking life had been black and white, and I didn't even realize it. Then one day she burst into my world, bringing every motherfucking shade of color with her." I shrug, resigned. "She makes my life better."

We lapse into silence, watching the people around us enjoying their night, while we finish our beers.

"We're a couple of fucking pussies, aren't we?"

Nodding vehemently, Ben's reply is instantaneous. "Yes, yes we are."

In an unspoken agreement we begin to move toward the entrance of the bar, when suddenly a voice that causes my dick to stiffen, and Ben to flinch simultaneously, calls out to us.

"Spanky! Where you going? Skyeballs needs your baaaaaalls!"

"Oh my god, Cassidy, *stop!*" Turning, I spot my demonic girlfriend headed toward us, evil dancing in her eyes. A very embarrassed Skye is following close behind, flanked by a petite blonde and a leggy redhead.

Cassidy throws herself into my arms as soon as she's close enough, peppering kisses along my jaw.

"Did you miss me, Sunshine?" Over her shoulder I see Ben wrap Skye up in a hug while nodding a hello to her friends. Looking down, and focusing back on Cassidy, I place a soft kiss on her forehead.

"How many drinks have you had, Crazy?"

"Three," she replies, holding up four fingers. "Oh! Mason! You need to meet my baby sister!" Her voice is loud, and she's gaining attention from the crowd around us, but she's oblivious, and I couldn't care less. My girl is cute as fuck when she's drunk.

"Lay! Bubs come here!" She yanks on the hand of the blonde and pulls her over to us, wrapping an arm around her tightly. "This is Layla." The pride in her voice is undeniable. As is the deep flush on Layla's cheeks.

I reach out a hand to her. "It's great to finally meet you, Layla. I'm sorry that I had to skip out on dinner last week."

"Oh, don't worry about it, things happen. And it's nice to meet you, too." Her voice is soft, I have to strain to hear her, but it's sweet.

I can't help but notice the contrast in the sister's appearance. Cassidy is all long limbs, creamy pale skin and big, blue eyes; while Layla is tiny, only coming up to Cassidy's shoulders. She has the type of skin that looks perpetually sunkissed, and while her eyes match Cassidy's in size, hers are a deep, chocolate brown. While they're both stunning, it really is remarkable that they're sisters.

"Oh, and this is Red," Cassidy gestures with her head to the fourth member of their group. "And you know Skyeballs."

Red steps toward me, throwing Cassidy an indulgent smile.

"Hi, Mason, I'm Wyatt, it's so nice to finally meet you."

"C'mon, let's get inside, I'm freezing my tush off out here." Skye plants a kiss on my cheek as she walks past, making her way into the pub, followed by Ben and Wyatt.

"After you, ladies."

"Pfft, see, Lay, you think he's being a gentleman, but he really just wants to check out my ass." She turns to me. "I'm on to you, mister. But since you have a supremely talented tongue, and a spectacular cock, I'll let it slide." With that she sashays into the pub, leaving me stunned. Just the way she likes it.

Hours later, I'm watching my girlfriend up on the bar dancing her heart out with her best friends, and a group of women she barely knows.

The arrival of Cassidy and Skye had Jack, the birthday boy, on the phone to his girlfriend, Shayne, who then met us here with her friends.

Cassidy's outgoing nature had the two groups of girls acting like long lost friends in no time, and that's how we find ourselves here. Seven women who are all some variance of drunk, dancing on a bar to old nineties pop songs.

The guys and I are all watching in awe, and as much as I love seeing Cassidy so happy, there is a part of me that's dreading tomorrow. I have a feeling that a hungover Cassidy is going to be an unpleasant Cassidy.

Ben and I sit side by side watching the show our girls are providing, but when Cassidy has a close call with the end of the bar, we agree that it might be time to call it a night.

Approaching the bar, Skye spots Ben first. "Baby-cakes!" Without a second thought, she jumps down into his arms, giggling. "Benjamin, I think I'm drunk!"

His answering smile is warm. "I think you might be right, Squeak. You want to go home?" He leans down and whispers something in her ear that has her blushing beet red before nodding enthusiastically. Ben laughs, and then turns to help Wyatt down.

"I'll get these girls home, and leave you to your handful. I'll see you on Sunday for the game?"

"Sounds good. I'll bring the beer."

"Fuck yeah, you will. The good stuff too, rich boy." I shake my head with a laugh. I'll never get used to that nickname. I say goodbye to Skye and Wyatt, but as they start to walk away, Cassidy screeches at them.

"Biatches! Where are you going?"

They turn back to her, but Ben shakes his head and keeps them moving forward.

"You suck, Spanky!"

"Alright, Crazy, time to go home." Layla left a couple of hours ago, so I'm left with just Cassidy to wrangle. My hand reaches out and takes hold of hers, but is met with total resistance.

"Nope, I wanna dance."

"Baby, you're drunk, it's not safe up there, come down."

"You know how many fucks I give, Sunshine?" She holds up her hand and makes a circle with her thumb and forefinger. "Zero! Zero fucks given, babe."

I reach up with both hands and take a firm grip of her hips, pulling her down to me and sitting her ass on the bar.

"We're going home." My voice is firm, making it clear that there's no room for disagreement.

Cassidy watches me with alcohol-hazed eyes, and then crooks her finger, motioning me toward her. I move without a thought, because it's Cassidy. I'll always go to her.

She reaches up and kisses my neck, her tongue snaking out to trace a path up to my ear, where she bites on my earlobe, sending a current of electricity straight to my dick.

"You know what, Sunshine?" Her whisper tickles my ear.

"What, Crazy?"

"I think I could love you forever." Her following sigh is deep, and she presses her forehead against my chest while my heart hammers at her confession.

For the first time I consider that perhaps our ending isn't inevitable.

"I hope so, baby. Now, let's go home."

CHAPTER THIRTEEN

*T*anya's head pops up as I enter Mason's offices, her face lighting up when she spots the cupcake box in my hands.

"Hey, Cass, what are you doing here?" Her voice is curious, but her eyes haven't moved from the box.

"I just need to speak to Mason for a minute, is he available?"

"Yeah, go on in, babe."

"Thanks, and this is for you." Opening the box, I pull out a lemon curd cupcake. "Your favorite."

"Oh my god, I *love* you!" Her hands grab the cupcake and start removing the outer paper immediately. "He's grumpy today, so perhaps you can cheer him up." Her eyebrows waggle.

I school my face into a look of innocence before responding.

"I have no idea what you mean."

"Sure, you don't. But on a completely unrelated

topic, would you like some privacy?" The smirk on her face leaves no doubt to what she means.

"Now that you mention it... I did bring a cupcake for Kim, but she wasn't at her desk. Maybe you could take it to her?" I hand her the chocolate orange fudge cake.

"You've got fifteen minutes," she says as she makes her way out. "So no foreplay."

Heeding her warning, I move quickly, making my way to Mason's door and walking through without announcing myself.

He glances up at me, sitting back in his chair and allowing his eyes to roam over my body. The heat in his gaze makes my – no! I won't be distracted by his deliciousness.

"You don't seem surprised to see me, Sunshine." Walking across the room, I stand in front of his desk, placing the box of treats down. My finger traces the new logo stamped on the box, *Frosted by Cassidy*, and I smile wickedly up at Mason.

"I may have gotten an email that tipped me off." His answering smirk is just as sinful.

"I received an offer today."

His arms fold across his chest. "You don't say. What kind of offer would that be?"

He wants to play it that way? No skin off my nose.

"The HR manager from Early Bird Productions called me and offered me a permanent contract. I would be supplying their offices with a daily order of cupcakes. Some of which will be used on their morning news show, you know the one? It has that weekly animal segment, where everything always goes wrong? It's fucking hilarious." I shake my head with a snort at the memory of last week's debacle when a tiny monkey lost its temper with one of the co-hosts and slapped her. "Anyway, I digress. They're going to use the cupcakes as a display, and credit me. How incredible is that?"

"It is pretty damn incredible, Crazy, but not surprising. You're talented." He says it as if it's nothing. As if getting an opportunity like this, with a steady income that still leaves me enough time to take on custom orders, is nothing. When the reality is, it's everything.

"You wouldn't happen to know anything about this would you?"

Throwing his pen down, he sighs as though expecting an argument from me. He's not going to get one.

"All I did was make a phone call, Cass. I heard that they were looking for a new bakery to supply them, so I called the president and put your name up for consideration. That order you made for us last week was sent over to him. But that was it. I didn't pull any strings, or cash in any favors. You got the contract on your own merits, I promise."

I roll my eyes. Jesus, this man. "I know, Sunshine. My cakes are fucking amazeballs, of course I got the contract." I rush around the desk, and sit myself on his lap, wiggling my ass against his cock as a little extra thank you. "Thank you." I look around the office that I've come to know so well, sunlight bouncing off the clean lines of the modern furnishings. "I start in three weeks." I feel his body tense under mine. "So, I guess I'm handing in my resignation."

"Right. Of course." His arms tighten around me, and there is an undeniable wave of melancholy that washes over us. Who would have thought I'd ever be sad at the idea of leaving an office job? But I know it's more than that.

I met my future here. My heart remembered how to beat here, and I'm so sad to say goodbye.

We're snapped out of our pensiveness by a door slamming in the outer office, and Tanya calling out, "I'm back! I hope everyone has pants on!" Seconds later her head pops around the door. "You have that conference call in twenty minutes, Mason." His arms remain unmoving, not even trying to hide his affection from Tanya. I soak in his comfort for a few moments, before pushing away and patting his chest.

"I'm going to head home, I had an idea for a new flavor that I want to experiment with. Are you going to come by my place after?" His expression is wistful, and for a fleeting second a sense of panic trickles through my blood.

"Yeah, I shouldn't be too late." My body relaxes at his words, and after a final goodbye, I make my way home.

Music blares from my phone and I shake my ass exuberantly as I sing along to Rhianna's *S&M*, keeping time as I mix up a bowl of frosting.

My apartment is warm, and I've built up a slight sweat with all my dancing, so I'm wearing very little. A pair of black lacy boy-shorts are displaying my ass, in all its booty-shaking glory, and a simple white tank completes my look. Very fashion forward, if I do say so myself.

My body stills as I feel the heat of someone standing behind me, and a glance over my shoulder confirms that Mason has arrived.

"Hey, Sunshine."

He presses his body flush against my back, and what should feel suffocating instead fills me with desire.

His mouth gently grazes my neck before his teeth nip my earlobe causing me to bite down on my bottom lip to suppress a moan.

"Why was the door unlocked, Crazy?" His voice is nothing but a whisper, however the dominance he still manages to convey has my thighs clenching.

Using my hips, I turn myself around so that I am facing him.

"I knew you were coming, it's not a big deal."

"Am I?"

My face twists in confusion. "Are you what?"

"Am I going to be coming?" I don't even bother to try and stop my scornful response..

"C'mon, Sunshine. You're better than that." A deep, throaty chuckle rumbles through him.

"I am. I apologize." Lowering his head until his lips are a breath away from my ear, he whispers, "Lock your damn door, baby." He moves forward slightly, his firm chest brushing my breasts, as he reaches for something behind me. All I can focus on is the tiny fireworks exploding in all my most favorite places. Keeping my gaze locked on his, I notice too late that he has swiped a finger full of buttercream frosting, and he shoves it in his lush mouth, sucking it clean. Such a greedy fucker.

"Mason! I'm going to have to make another batch now, you douche nozzle!" His answering smirk manages to both piss me off and make my pussy pulse simultaneously.

"Well, that's a shame." Although he sounds anything but regretful. "But we can't let this go to waste. That would be a damn travesty." His eyes trail down my body, and I swear to all that is holy, I feel it. Just as surely as if it was a finger gliding along my skin, setting my body alight.

"You won't be needing this," he pulls my tank up over my head and tosses it over his shoulder, leaving me almost completely exposed.

I can feel the wetness in my panties, and know that if he looked right now, my thighs would glisten with my arousal, begging for his tongue to taste me.

He takes a moment to observe, and fuck if I don't love his eyes on me.

His finger dips back into the bowl of frosting, but instead of letting that talented tongue of his taste the sweet goodness once again, I watch as it descends toward my breast, slowly. Deliberately. As soon as he makes contact a deep groan escapes me, and as his finger trails a delicious path, painting my nipples with the sugary goodness, the throbbing in my clit increases until it's almost painful.

I squeeze my thighs together in an effort to subdue the intensity, but as his mouth devours me, licking, sucking, tasting, I realize that it's hopeless.

Then his teeth close around my nipple, biting down until the pain gives way to the most intense kind of pleasure, and it's on. It's on like fucking Donkey Kong.

My hands are frenzied as they claw at his clothes, desperate for the feel of his skin beneath them.

He pauses his relentless assault, and a shiver runs through my body at the loss of his heat. In minutes he has his jacket, tie and shirt removed and I graze my fingertips across his chest, enjoying the sensation of hard muscle and the light smattering of chest hair underneath them.

A feral moan from Mason has my eyes drifting back up to his face, delighting in the lack of control he has when it comes to me. The power I feel when a man as in control as he always is, loses his shit, all because of me, is intoxicating.

Pushing him back, I fall to my knees, the hard surface of the floor not even registering as my hands go to his zipper, dragging it down. This sound, and Mason's ragged breathing, are all I can hear, despite the music blaring in the background. I am completely fixated on the man in front of me.

Pulling his tailored dress pants down I come face to

face with my favorite cock of all time. I call him Winky. But never in front of Mason. He was *not* impressed the one time I did. So for now, it's mine and Winky's little secret.

He's already fully hard, with a tiny drop of pre-cum on the tip that is just begging to be licked clean.

Leaning forward, I swipe my tongue across it, loving the way it jerks at my touch. My lips close around the head, licking and sucking before sliding further down, taking as much of him in as I can. Which isn't as much as I would like. My man was blessed with length *and* width. Go me!

My head starts bobbing, my mouth pooling with saliva as I taste him.

His hands lash out, knocking the iPod docking station over before taking hold of the kitchen counter.

The room is now silent except for the erotic sounds of my mouth on his cock. He is slightly bent over me, and as I look up at him, my pace never faltering, I am slayed by the look of lust in his eyes.

Allowing him to pop free of my mouth, I continue to jerk him off while I move down and lick his balls, gently sucking them into my mouth, and giving the boys the attention they deserve.

Moving back up, my tongue plays with his head, while I use my hands to pump his shaft.

"Fuuuck, Crazy, you look so fucking beautiful with your mouth full of my cock. I'm close, baby. I'm gonna come in your mouth and you're gonna swallow it all down for me, yeah? Every last drop, like a good girl."

My eyes start to water as Mason loses all semblance

of control and starts thrusting into my mouth. I can feel him growing even larger, and my pussy is throbbing at the sounds coming out of his mouth.

Mason's hands thread through my hair and I allow him to take over, as my own hand drops to my clit. Applying pressure I start to feel my orgasm build, and my moans mingle with his.

He comes with a roar, and as his cum slides down my throat, I finger my piercing, twisting my nipple, and that's all it takes to tip me over the edge.

His dick slips from my mouth, and we are both completely still as we try to catch our breath.

When my vision seems to have come back into focus, I look up at him, my eyes filled with mischief.

"So, how was your day, honey?"

"So, do you kids have any plans for Thanksgiving yet?"

"Oh Jesus, subtle, Mom." I groan as my mother widens her eyes innocently, as if she has no clue what I'm talking about. Mason sits beside her, his shoulders shaking in a silent laugh, so I fix him with a glare.

"Uh, no we haven't really discussed it, Laura." His voice shakes with humor, but I can feel my parents tense up on either side of us.

Holidays are a big deal in my family. Layla comes home from college, and our family of four is joined by aunts, uncles and cousins. Sometimes even family friends. It's seriously crazy, but I love every second of it.

I can see my mother's eyes crease with worry at the thought of me being absent from the festivities, but I don't know how to reassure her. Mason and I haven't talked about this, and we've only been together a few months, but I don't want to hurt him by assuming spending the day together isn't something he would want.

Mason has clearly picked up on my mom's concerns, but as always, he is straight to the point, and lays his cards on the table.

"I would love to spend the day with Cassidy, but I do understand that Thanksgiving is a day for family. I'm sure we'll come up with a plan." Swinging his gaze back to me, he continues, "Maybe we can have a late dinner, or spend the Friday together."

"Yep, sounds like a plan, Sunshine." I throw my mom a look to say *'see, nothing to worry about!'* but her eyes are fixed on Mason, oblivious to me.

"Mason, why don't you and your mother join us?" I had filled my parents in on his family situation before this meeting, in the hopes that my mother wouldn't blurt out anything embarrassing. I'm not sure what exactly, but as much as I love her, she has a way of sticking her foot in her mouth without even trying.

"It really is a free-for-all at our house on Thanksgiving. Everyone is welcome, and we would love to meet your mother."

My father nods his approval. "Absolutely, the more the merrier. You are both very welcome to join us." He reaches out and squeezes my hand. "I know Bunny would love it."

Mason quirks an eyebrow at me across the table, and I roll my eyes, shaking my head. *Thanks for that, Dad.*

"That would be great. I'll need to check with Mom, but I'm sure she would love to. I think she loves Cassidy more than me at this point, so she'll be thrilled."

"Pfft, of course she does. I'm fucking awesome."

"Cassidy Grace! Language please, young lady." My mother's voice is stern and Mason smirks at me while shaking his head in mock disappointment.

We spend a few more minutes discussing Thanksgiving plans when we are interrupted by the ring of Mason's cell phone.

Discreetly checking the caller ID, he apologizes to my parents before moving away from the table to take the call.

Returning a few minutes later, he lets us know that a situation has arisen at the office and apologizes profusely for his early exit.

"Do you need me to come back, too?" He seems rattled, and my spidey senses are tingling.

Coming up behind me, he leans down and places a soft kiss on my neck, just below my ear.

"No, you stay and enjoy the rest of your meal. William, Laura," he nods at my parents, "it was so nice to finally meet you both. Thank you for the Thanksgiving invitation, I'm sure I'll see you again soon." With a final gentle squeeze to my shoulders, he takes off with a sense of urgency.

"I like him, Cassidy."

I turn to my father. "Hmm?" Distracted by Mason's hasty retreat, and the sense of foreboding I'm struck with, I miss his comment.

"I like him. I think he's just the type of man you need. He'll hold his own." A smile plays on my lips at my dad's seal of approval.

"You have no idea, Dad."

❧

Forty-five minutes later I enter the office with a takeout bag for Mason in my hands. I even brought him a piece of red velvet cake, which I'm hopeful his tongue will thank me for tonight.

Reaching my desk, I place the food down and am just placing my purse in my bottom drawer when the door to Mason's office bursts open and Mr. Thompson comes flying out.

He almost storms out without even noticing me, which I probably would have preferred. The douche nugget gives me the creeps.

I'm not that lucky, though, and he stops dead in his tracks, turning and squinting his weasley little eyes at me.

"Cassidy Jensen?"

"Yes, Mr Thompson. It's so nice to see you again." Oh God, somebody gag me. "How have you been?"

His face twists into a look of pure anger, and I'm left completely bewildered.

"Well, I guess it makes more sense now. You should be ashamed of yourself. What you've done is unforgivable, I don't know how you live with yourself." My jaw drops as he turns on his heel and continues storming out.

Turning my head, I spot Mason standing in his doorway with an unreadable expression on his face.

"What the actual fuck, Sunshine?"

otherfucker.
My hand drags through my hair as I try to understand what the hell just happened.

"What the fuck was that about?" Cassidy's voice cuts through my shock, and I hate what I'm about to tell her.

"Come in here, Cassidy." She hesitates, still standing in the same position she was in when Thompson began his attack. After a beat, she stalks into my office.

"What was he talking about, Mason." Her voice is low and surprisingly controlled. I have an inkling this will be her ultra-angry voice when our kids piss her off. *Kids? What the fuck, let's not get ahead of ourselves, asshole.*

"It seems someone used the cheating information to..." my voice trails off. There's really no good way to finish this sentence. "To compel Alistair to sign the contract."

Her body is rigid, and her face bright red. It's an

interesting contrast to her pink hair. Although, that's not probably something I should be considering right now.

"You used the information I told you to *blackmail* someone?" Disbelief drips from every syllable. "How the fuck could you do that?"

"No, of course I didn't." I try my best to keep the defensive tone out of my voice, but it's a fucking failure.

"Well then how the fuck did this happen? Jesus, Mason, I told you that in *bed*, you megacuntwaffleass-wipe! I *never* would have told you if I knew I couldn't trust you." The rage emanating from her is palpable, and my anxiety ratchets up a notch.

"You *can* trust me. *I* didn't do this."

"But you know who did." It's not a question. It's an accusation. And I have no defence, because I do.

"I thought I could trust Stella." Even to my own ears that sounds ridiculous now. She's an absolute shark and does whatever it takes to get the job done. It's why she's so lethal to go up against.

"Your fuck buddy? You told your motherfucking fuck buddy something I told you in confidence?"

"Obviously I didn't know she was going to use the information, Cassidy."

"Didn't you?" The accusation is quick and punches me in the gut. Of course I didn't. *Did I?*

"I don't do this, Mason." Regret laces her voice. "I don't shit over people's lives just to make a buck. What you've done, and you did play a part in this, don't kid yourself that you didn't, it disgusts me." She shakes her head, and I can see her trying to figure out how we got here. I wish I had an answer for her.

"I'm done." She spins around and storms toward the door.

Are you fucking kidding me?

"Are you fucking kidding me? What the hell does that even mean?"

Swinging around, venom oozes from every fiber of her being.

"It *means* that I'm done. I don't work here anymore. And you need to stay away from me until I calm down and figure out what I want to do."

"You're being fucking ridiculous. The guy's an asshole. If he could keep his dick in his pants this wouldn't even be a discussion. It's his own fucking fault." As soon as the words leave my mouth I realize my mistake.

"If you believe that, you're not the person I thought you were." And then she's gone.

"Stella Daniels' office."

"Tre, put me through to Stella, please." I force the words out through clenched teeth.

"Of course, Mr. Alexander. One moment please." My ears are briefly filled with shitty music before my call connects.

"Mason, what can I do for you?" There is no hint of unease in her voice. No hint that she might have just majorly fucked up. Only effortless confidence.

"What the fuck did you do, Stella?" I'm having trouble controlling my anger. Worse still, I'm having trouble caring.

Her answering sigh is one of exasperation.

"I did what you couldn't, Mason. I closed an account that should have been closed months ago. I did what I needed to do." She pauses before continuing. "I did what *you* would have done four months ago. That pink-haired, crass excuse for an assistant of yours has made you soft."

My vision starts to blur, and my hand tightens around the phone. "What are you talking about?"

"Oh, please. Don't tell me you really think it was a secret? The entire building knows you're fucking your secretary, as cliché as it is. But, hey, it's none of our business if you want to slum it for a while."

"You fucking bitch."

"What are you really pissed about here, Mason? That you're no longer at the top of your game? Or is it that your Pink-wannabe side fuck is mad at you, and you're worried that you're not going to get a piece of that D-grade ass anymore?" I'm momentarily stunned speechless by her maliciousness. This isn't the cool, calm and collected Stella I'm used to dealing with.

"I'm *pissed*, Stella, because I told you something in confidence and you turned around and used the information to *blackmail* someone. It's fucking illegal!"

"Oh, for Christ's sake, Mason. I merely mentioned that I had seen him out with his lady friend, and *suggested* he may want to be a bit more discreet in the future. There were no threats, no cajoling. *No blackmail.*"

"The implication was there, Stella, and you fucking know it. I'm sorry, but I have no choice but to go to Jonathan about this."

"Go for it. I think you'll find that Mr. Cook is more than happy with my work." Her words are laced with arrogance, and I realize with complete certainty that this conversation is futile. My finger hovers over the end-call button, when her voice stops me.

"When you get tired of waiting around for your pussy pal, you have my num—"

My finger stabs my phone. End call.

Twenty minutes later my head is in my hands as the voice of Jonathan Cook, owner of Cook Enterprises, barks at me through the speakerphone.

"I took a huge risk appointing you as CEO, Mason. You're young, and you lack the experience that many of your fellow candidates had. But I was confident that your single-mindedness and determination would more than make up for that. Now, I'm not so sure." He's interrupted by someone, and there is the low whisper of voices, and paper shuffling. "Frankly, Mason, I feel like you've been off your game lately. Get your shit together, or we may need to revisit your appointment as chief executive officer of my company. Are we clear?"

My back straightens at his question, and the condescension in his voice causes my hackles to rise.

"Absolutely, Jonathan."

"Good. I hope things can get bac—"

"Jonathan? I quit." Before he can respond, I end the call.

Leaning back in my chair, I wait for the fear to hit me. For the anxiety that I may have just monumentally fucked up my life, to overwhelm me.

Instead all I feel is free.

Now I just need to get Cassidy to forgive me.

꧁꧂

"Wow." My mother has been completely silent as I filled her in on everything that's been going on in my life, and as I watch her now, I don't believe I've ever seen her so shocked.

"I'm proud of you, my sweet boy. I've been hoping you would finally come to your senses and start living your life for yourself, rather than for some ridiculous obligation to me."

My hands tighten around my coffee mug, and I flinch slightly at her words.

Had it been ridiculous? I look around my mother's tiny apartment full of used furnishings and well-loved knick-knacks. I only ever wanted to give her the life she deserved. One of comfort and beautiful things. The one she lost all hope of when she fell in love with an asshole and had me.

As if sensing where my thoughts are going, she places a hand on my forearm, and squeezes gently.

"I love that you wanted to take care of me. You have such a kind heart, Mason. But it's not a child's job to look after their parent; and I never could have allowed you to do so when I knew how miserable those choices were making you." Mom's eyes are soft, and full of love.

"Yeah, Cassidy helped me realize that what I was doing was pointless. Then when Stella pulled that shit, and Jonathan supported it, it was like a wake-up call." Bringing the mug to my lips, I swallow down some coffee. "The worst thing is, I'm not sure they're wrong. Six months ago, fuck, even four months ago, I might have used that information in exactly the same way." I gnaw on my bottom lip as I consider what I just said. "No, the worst thing is, I'm not convinced I didn't know what Stella would do with the information."

Mom sits silently, mulling over what I just confided.

"You can't change the past, sweetheart. Whether you did, or didn't, is irrelevant now. Make sure you've learned from it, though. Make it count for something." Taking my now empty mug from me, she moves to the kitchen sink, and places our dirty dishes inside.

"I don't know if Cassidy will be as forgiving." Two days after our confrontation, she's still refusing my calls.

Turning around, she crosses her arms across her chest and fixes me with a stern look. "It sounds like you have some wooing to do now, my boy."

A smile is playing on her lips, so I quirk an eyebrow at her. "Wooing?"

"Every woman likes to be wooed, Mason. If I only teach you one thing in this life, let it be that." Crossing the tiny space between us, she places a kiss on the top of my head, and pulls me in for a hug.

"I like her, Mason. She's a fierce little smartass, and

she's exactly what you need. So you make sure that you woo her ass off."

§◆

Running up the steps to Cassidy's apartment building, I grab the door before it closes behind the elderly lady ahead of me.

I'm nervous as I make my way to her floor. She's still ignoring my calls, leaving me frustrated. I can't understand where her head is right now, and I'm worried that if we don't actually come face to face, she's going to run.

We might have only been together a few months, but I know my girl. I know how scared she was to take a chance on this relationship, and I don't want her to use this as an excuse to retreat back to her former life of casual flings, as a way of avoiding getting hurt.

I reach her door, and my hands tighten around the small bouquet of daisies in my hands. Taking a deep breath, I knock.

There is the sound of movement inside, and then the gentle thud of hands landing on the door. I imagine her on the other side, looking through the peephole, and I will her silently to open the door.

Nothing. The door remains unmoving.

"Cassidy." Her soft sigh is audible through the door, and it urges me on. "Open the door, Crazy. We need to figure this out, and that's not going to happen through a door." Silence is her only response.

"I fucked up, Cassidy, I warned you I would, and I'm

sure it won't be the last time I do. But we need to talk so we can move past it. Your stubborn ass needs to talk to me." There is a huff of indignation from inside the apartment, and I smirk at the sound.

"Let me in, Crazy."

"I can't. Not yet. I'm sorry."

Fuck.

"You remember that night I told you I owned you? Well, I was wrong. You fucking own me, Crazy, and I'm not letting you go without a fight. I can out stubborn your ass any day of the week. So, I'll leave, but I will be back."

Placing the flowers by her door, I turn and walk away, already plotting my next move.

CHAPTER FIFTEEN

CASSIDY

"*I*t's such a beautiful day," Layla's voice is all dreamy as she lies on the blanket, arms behind her head, gazing up at the clear blue sky.

We're in the park behind my parent's house, enjoying a picnic on this beautiful Fall day. The sun is shining, taking the bite out of the crisp air, and I'm feeling more relaxed than I have in days.

"Mmm, it really is, this was a great idea, Cass." Skye's head is lying in my lap. "How's the kitchen search going?"

A small smile graces my lips, and the sensation almost feels weird. I haven't been smiling too much lately. "Great, actually. I think I've found something."

Skye bolts up, and Layla and Wyatt both turn my way.

"That's fantastic, sweetie! Where is it?" Wyatt questions.

"It's only nine blocks from my place, which is great. It's only a small commercial kitchen, but it's big enough for what I need. It even has a small shop front so I'm going to put in some display cases and sell a small selection of cupcakes every day." I grimace. "Well, hopefully sell them, anyway."

I sit quietly as my girls gush over me, but I struggle to match their enthusiasm. I wasn't supposed to be doing this by myself, and every decision I make, every milestone I achieve just reminds me what, or who, is missing.

"You were so lucky you got that business loan, CJ."

"Pfft, fuck luck, Lay. Between my savings, the contract I have and the business plan Spanky helped me with, they had no choice but to say yes."

"It was pretty impressive, even Ben thought so." Ah, Skyeballs. She always has my back.

"How are you doing with everything else, Cassidy?" Wyatt asks.

It's been two weeks since my fight with Mason. Two of the longest fucking weeks of my life. He's turned up at my apartment a few times, but it always ends in a silent stand-off before he finally leaves. I guess I proved who is the most stubborn. Despite my continued silence, he calls every day, sometimes more than once, and always leaves a message. I haven't listened to any of them; I just can't yet. Skye keeps urging me to talk to him, telling me there's things I need to know, but refusing to tell me what. Which only serves to piss me off.

"I'm getting by, Red. That's really all I've got right now." My voice is tinged with sadness.

"When are you going to hear him out, CJ?" My head

snaps to Layla, and I can't contain my shock at her tone.

"What the hell is up your nose?"

"What did he do that was so freaking bad?" Layla's brow is furrowed, and her mouth pursed. So, this is what my baby sister looks like pissed.

"He took something I told him, and he used it to play God with somebody's life, Layla. *That's* what he did."

"No, he didn't. He told someone he thought he could trust. *He* did exactly what *you* did when *you* told *him*. You can't hold him responsible for what that person did."

Skye and Wyatt's eyes are wide and bouncing between the two of us. This is not usual behavior for the Jensen sisters.

"He knew what she would do." I see Skye shake her head in the periphery of my vision, and my temper flares even further. "He knew."

"Did he? Or are you sabotaging your first real relationship since Aidan died?" My sharp intake of breath is instinctual, and I hear a gasp to my left; but Layla ignores our reaction and rushes on. "You and Aidan barely knew each other, Cassidy. You spent four months getting drunk together, and fucking each other in random places on campus. I know you thought you loved him. I know you thought losing him broke you. But if you don't fix things with Mason, I think you'll find out what broken really feels like." Gathering up her things, Layla mutters goodbye to the others, before turning her attention back to me. "Don't mess this up,

CJ. You'll always regret it if you do." With that she turns and stalks off as quickly as her little legs will take her.

We sit there in silence for a while, all of us digesting what just happened.

"I always knew she would explode one day." Wyatt's voice is matter-of-fact, and we all burst out laughing.

"What the hell *was* that?" I exclaim. Skye and Wyatt share a look that has my defences rising. "What?"

"Okay, don't hate us, Cass, but could she have a point? I think we all figured you two would be back together by now. I'm not quite sure why you're being so stubborn about this?" Wyatt is nodding her head in agreement. "He asks Ben about you every time he sees him. I'm sorry, Cass, but I think you're being unfair."

"How can I trust him again, after what he did?"

"Cassidy, you're overreacting." Wyatt's voice is firm. "I think you fell in love with him, and you got scared. So now you're leaving him before he leaves you."

"Or is taken from you," Skye interrupts.

"No." I shake my head vehemently. "No, I have every right to be angry about this."

"Of course you do. But this is not an end-your-relationship obstacle, Cassidy. This is a blowout fight, silent treatment for a few days and then crazy-makeup-sex obstacle. Sweetie, you're punishing yourself right along with him. And honestly? Neither of you deserve it."

"You love him, Cass." Skye moves over behind me, and wraps her arms around me. "He lit you up, babes.

He brought your sunshine back. Please don't give up on him."

Feeling completely rattled, I close my eyes. "I think I need to be alone."

Shifting my gaze to my two best friends, I can see them struggle with this. We don't leave each other. We're like the three fucking musketeers. Only hotter. But I need them gone right now.

"Please. I'm fine, I just need some time to think."

"Okay, but promise you'll call us if you need us?" Wyatt's face is lined with concern.

"Of course I will. Now get your asses out of here. I'll probably call you later to organize a girls' night. It's been a while."

"I'd really like that, Cass." Skye kisses my cheek, and Wyatt reaches out and gives my hand a squeeze.

I watch them walk away, and then lie down staring up at the sky, contemplating what just went down. They have no idea what it's like to lose someone you love with every part of yourself. Despite what Layla thinks, I loved Aidan as completely as I could. Yes, it might not have been a mature love, but it was powerful just the same. And the torment I've felt after only a couple of weeks away from Mason, frightens me intensely. If I'm in this much pain after only a few months with him, how devastated would I be if it ends six months from now. Or a year? Or five? I don't think I could live through that.

My phone is wrapped tightly in my palm, and I run my thumb across the screen, bringing it up in front of my face. Scrolling to Mason's name, my finger lingers over the call button, but for some reason I just can't push it.

"FUCK!" I throw my phone down, wishing it would crash into a thousand pieces. Instead, it merely bounces silently on the blanket, before lying there taunting me.

Turning my head away from it, I come face to face with a dandelion, and before I even consider what I'm doing, I pick it.

Closing my eyes, I make a wish and blow as the tears start to fall.

Two months later...

"Oh shit!" Sliding the tray into the display case, I grab a pair of tongs and right the cupcake that tipped over. Thank god, the little fucker is salvageable.

Standing straight, I stretch tall in an attempt to loosen my muscles after being hunched over in the kitchen all morning.

I'm full of pride as I look around my small bakery. Can I call it a bakery? It's a tiny shop front, only thirteen square feet, but it's big enough for what I want. One long display case is the most prominent feature of the shop. It holds about four dozen cupcakes, and I have been selling out most days. Foot traffic along this street has proven to be a godsend.

My days have fallen into a routine that I find exhausting, which suits me just fine. I spend seven hours a day baking for Early Bird Productions and this place, starting at five in the morning, then open the store from twelve until six. By the time I make it home, I'm ready to fall into bed, so I can do it all over again the next day.

Moving across the floor, I head for the door to flip the open sign around, when I am pulled up short by a couple walking past my window.

Mason.

With some whorefaced wench by his side. Okay, maybe that's a bit harsh, she actually looks quite sweet. But what the fuck? He's dating already?

They're laughing as they walk by, and he looks so fucking happy that the last little piece of my heart still standing, crumbles.

After a month, his daily calls, and subsequent messages, dwindled to once a week. I've never listened to any of them, but I can't bring myself to delete them. Because everyone was right. I regret letting him go. I miss his presence in my life. His body pressed up against mine at night. The way he made me laugh. Our fights. I miss it all.

My eyes are locked to the front window as if Mason is going to reappear, and the desire to hear his voice is suddenly overwhelming.

Rushing back to the kitchen, I grab my purse and pull my phone out. In seconds I have his last voicemail pulled up, and my heart is thundering in my chest, as I wait for his deep, rumbling voice to fill my ear.

"Hey, Crazy. How was your week? Mine was busy, I had my first—" My heart stutters as his voice cuts off and all

I can hear is the hum of background noise. *"You know what? I can't do this anymore, Cassidy, I'm sorry. I still can't quite believe you just threw us away like you did. I thought we had a future. I wanted that future with you. Fuck, I still want that future with you. But you've made it pretty fucking clear that you're done, and I'm sick of having a relationship with your phone."* A scratching noise sounds, and I imagine him dragging a hand along his scruff, a habit he always had when he was frustrated. Sadness courses through every fiber of my body. *"Be happy, Crazy. I love you."*

CHAPTER SIXTEEN

MASON

Three months later

My fingers race over my phone's keyboard, typing out an idea that just popped into my head for a research paper I'm working on.

Going back to college has proven to be a lot easier than I had anticipated. Ten years ago, my college life revolved around getting drunk at frat parties, getting laid by pretty girls, and busting my ass to excel in courses that I hated.

These days I'm studying something that I'm passionate about, and feeling good about the direction my life is taking.

Professionally, at least.

Glancing up, I look around the restaurant Ben picked out. Usually Sundays are spent at his and Skye's apartment, watching football. Apparently, Skye kicked us out today, because her book club was having an emergency meeting. Why the fuck a book club needs an emergency meeting is beyond me. Skye's only explanation was that we're men, so we wouldn't understand.

I'm not sure why we're having lunch here instead of just moving our plans to my place, but Ben was insistent, and he's paying so I'm letting it slide.

I check my watch, noting that he's late. I'm about to text him when I notice the hostess heading my way.

However, it's the cotton-candy-colored hair I spot behind her that has my hand stilling, and the breath leaving my body.

Coming to a stop in front of the table, the hostess moves slightly, fully revealing Cassidy to me, and giving her her first glimpse of me.

Her eyes widen, and her jaw drops in horror. I can see every thought that flits through her mind, and I know she's about to bolt.

My body tenses as I consider how I can stop her, when both of our phones buzz.

Cassidy pulls her phone out of her purse, quickly scanning the message, and then her head pops up and she scans the room, scowling.

I follow her line of sight and spot Ben and Skye seated at a table, on the other side of the restaurant.

Skye is glaring at Cassidy, and motioning her to sit down, while Ben sits back as if settling in for a show.

I glance down at my phone and read the message I received.

. . .

Ben: You're welcome.

"Ma'am, is there a problem?"

The hostess's voice draws our attention back to her.

"No, it's fine, thank you." A breath I didn't realize I was holding rushes out as Cassidy takes a seat opposite me.

Handing us our menus, the hostess lets us know a waiter will be by soon to take our order, and wishes us a nice meal.

With her departure, silence descends on us. I can't stop staring at her, and it's probably completely creepy, but I can't make myself care. It's been almost six months since I saw her, or even heard her voice.

She totally ghosted me, just disappeared from my life without a word. And even though I've spent the last six months missing everything about her, now that she's sitting in front of me I'm pissed as fuck.

"Well, isn't this just punch-you-in-the-face awkward." She throws this out with a half-smile.

"Almost as awkward as standing in an empty hallway, talking to a door." I shrug. "Or having a one-sided conversation with a voicemail. Or better yet, as awkward as a florist calling you to tell you your flowers were 'undeliverable'. Yeah, awkward sucks." She visibly flinches at my words.

"I…" her voice trails off, she looks completely lost, and it slays me. I'm about to apologize for my attack, when her eyes flash to life. Ah, there's my Crazy.

"You moved on," she hisses forcefully. "Yes, I

handled the situation badly. You messed up, and I messed up, but let's not pretend you were heartbroken about it."

What the fuck is she talking about? I haven't seen anyone since her. Hell, I haven't gotten laid since her. I'm pretty damn sure I have the worst case of blue balls that has ever existed.

"I don't know where you're getting your inform—"

"I saw you." Looking down, she's angrily playing with her napkin. "I saw you with another girl. It was right after you left your last message."

My mind works to place the moment she's talking about, and when it does, I shake my head in disbelief.

"My cousin. That was my cousin, Kerry. She was visiting from Chicago." Cassidy bites down on her bottom lip, worrying it back and forth.

"Oh. So, not a girlfriend then."

We are interrupted by the arrival of the waiter, and spend a few awkward moments listening to the specials and placing our orders before we are once again left to ourselves.

"You really thought I would move on that quickly?" How could she think so little of me?

Cassidy shakes her head, and shrugs. "Why wouldn't you? I was an assmunch. I treated you like shit."

"Yeah, you did. Got an explanation for that, Crazy?"

She takes her time answering, and I let my gaze wander around the restaurant before landing on Skye and Ben, who both have their eyes glued to our table.

"Look at them." I huff out a laugh. "Those fuckers

178

just need some popcorn and they'll be set." Her answering laugh lifts a weight off my shoulders. I've missed that sound.

"We're going to have to punish them for this, you realize that, right? I'm thinking we put some jolly ranchers in their shower head and give them a nice sticky shower."

"Jesus," I laugh. "You take way too much pleasure in tormenting people."

I pause, before deciding to continue. "I don't really want to punish them. They managed to do what I couldn't. Get you in the same room as me."

"I'm sorry." She holds my eye, and I can see the regret in them. "I got scared. I never intended to break up with you, but I was *so* fucking angry. I was *so* pissed at you. Then the longer I left it to talk to you, the harder it became to reach out." She lets out a deep sigh. "I realized how vulnerable you made me. How easily you could hurt me. And I was a fucking pussy and I ran away. I'm sorry I did that."

I consider her words. She hasn't said anything I didn't already know. I knew why she did what she did. I even understood it. I just didn't have a way to convince her she was wrong. I won't let that happen again.

"So how is my replacement working out, Sunshine? I bet she doesn't keep you on your toes like I did." I smirk at her sass.

"No one keeps me on my toes like you do, Crazy." I take a sip from my water glass. "I quit."

She looks up in confusion. "What?"

179

"I quit. What they did crossed a line, fucking with people's lives like that, including mine. I couldn't stay there."

"Well, shit. What are you doing now?" Her eyes are alight with curiosity, and I am excited that I'm finally able to share this with her.

"I just started back at college. I'm doing a Bachelor of Science, so I can move into social work." I can't control the smile that spreads across my face. It's the same every time, no matter how many times I say it.

"Oh my god, that's... incredible! I'm so proud of you."

"What about you? How's *Frosted by Cassidy* going?" I lose my easy smile as a thought crosses my mind. "Did you keep the name?"

"Of course I did. It's still perfect." She shrugs. "It's going amazing actually. I'm still working with the television production team, and my private orders have increased consistently since I opened my shop."

"Wait, you have a shop?"

Smiling proudly, she replies, "Well, it's just a tiny little one. It's like the chihuahua of shops." She laughs. "But it's really helped me build the catering side of the business, so it does the job."

The arrival of our food puts a stop to immediate conversation. Cassidy groans at the sight of the burger in front of her.

"God, there's nothing better than a good burger." Her hands are already gripping the sandwich and bringing it to her mouth.

"I do recall you always liked a mouthful of meat."

The joke rolls off my tongue without even a thought, and Cassidy almost chokes as she laughs, spitting out tiny morsels of burger before covering her mouth. Fuck, my girl is all class.

We spend the rest of the meal catching each other up on our news, and it's the most enjoyable hour I've had since the last time she was under me, with my cock buried deep inside her. Shit, don't go there yet, Alexander.

"This has been fun, Sunshine. I'm glad we can stay friends, I've missed you." My drink stills its path to my mouth, and I take in her hopeful eyes.

Placing my glass back on the table, I lean forward so she hears me, and hears me good. "Fuck friends, Crazy. You and I will *never* be just friends. We will be everything. We're going to spend the rest of our lives loving, fucking and fighting with each other." I raise an eyebrow, challenging her. "Do you have a problem with that, Crazy?"

A smirk plays on her full mouth. "Not in the slightest, Sunshine. In fact, I would be happy to reacquaint myself with the fucking right now."

"Right now?" My gaze moves to our surroundings, taking in the busy restaurant. "I mean we may get arrested, but it'd be totally worth it."

Her laugh is loud and wild, the one that involves her entire body, and never fails to make me smile.

"How about we wait until we get to my place? Then you can go to town and do all the dirty things you want to me. Princess has had no action for six months. She missed Winky."

AMALI ROSE

"Christ, Cassidy." I feel my balls shrivel at the sound of that name. "Don't call my dick Winky, for the love of God, woman." I motion to the waiter for the check.

"So, we're doing this?" I look across the table at her, her uncertainty plain to see. "We're just going to act like the last six months never happened?"

"I love you. Do you love me?" My voice is confident, because I know the answer, and I know how this is going to play out.

"Yes." There's not a note of doubt in her voice.

"Then yeah, we're going to pretend the last six months never happened, and we're going to start our life. You good with that?"

"Fuck yeah, Sunshine, let's do it."

The waiter arrives, and I point him in the direction of Ben and Skye, who appear to have lost interest in our little show, and are currently making out. Christ, those two lack any kind of self-control.

"You see those two over there? The ones indulging in the over-the-top PDA? They'll be taking care of our check."

Cassidy and I quickly gather up our things, and as we prepare to leave I lace my fingers through hers and tilt her chin up until she's meeting my gaze.

"Why should they get all the fun?" My mouth slants down over hers, and she opens for me easily, our tongues lazily sliding against each other as her body melts into mine. I feel my cock start to harden, and she pushes her hips forward, pressing against me.

Pulling away before I get too carried away in the

middle of a crowded restaurant, I look down at her. "You ready to get forever started, Crazy?"

Her eyes glint wickedly. "Sunshine, I think the question is, are *you* ready?"

As we make our way through to the door, I look over at our best friends and see them watching us with giant smiles on their faces.

Turning back to Cassidy, I see her flipping them the bird, and a laugh rumbles through me.

Fuck yeah, I'm ready.

EPILOGUE

MASON

ne Year Later

"Ohmygodohmygodohmygodohmygod! Mason, I am going to cut your dick off. I swear to fucking Channing Tatum if you ever look at me with even the hint of a horndog look, your dick is gone. Do you hear me, Sunshine? Gone! Aaaaaaaahhhhhhh!"

I hold tight to Cassidy's hand, and take the abuse that she's heaping on me, happily. My eyes are glued to the corner of the room where a nurse is hovering over a tiny little shrieking bundle, cleaning her up. She definitely got her mother's lungs.

A sharp tug on my hand draws my attention right back to my wife, and I lean my head down, placing my forehead against her temple. Our hands are joined, and I bring our fused fist to my mouth and kiss her knuckles. Her face is bright red and covered in a sheen of sweat, her blonde hair sticking all over, but fuck if she isn't as beautiful as she was the day I met her.

"Okay, Cassidy, you're doing great. A couple more pushes and the baby will be here." The doctor calls out from between her legs.

"Aaaahhh fuuuuuuck! I already had a baby, uuuughh, this one's just going to have to stay in!" Cassidy starts crying and reaches around, pulling my head even closer to her. "I can't do this, Mason, please, babe, I can't, I'm so fucking tired, please make it stop," she cries.

"Crazy, listen to me, you're doing an amazing job. I'm so fucking proud of you." Her face is streaked with tears, and it scrunches with pain as another contraction washes over her. The doctor instructs her to push, and my girl gives it her all, pushing with everything she has.

Suddenly a wail echoes around the room, and there's a hive of activity down below. The doctor raises his voice to be heard above the din, "It's a boy, Cassidy. You have a girl and a boy."

She slumps back down on the bed, exhausted, sobs wracking her body.

"It's done? I can stop now?"

"Yeah, baby, you can stop. You did so good, our babies are here."

"Are they okay? Mason, why can't I stop crying? I want my babies, Mase." Her words are soft and muffled, and I have trouble understanding her, but those azure eyes are as emotive as always, so I pull her to me in an uncomfortable embrace, doing my best to comfort her, as I feel the unmistakable sting of my own tears.

A gentle touch on my shoulder has me looking around to see a nurse standing beside me holding my daughter.

"Are you ready to hold your daughter, Cassidy?"

Tears are still running silently down her cheeks as she nods, holding her arms out, and I watch in awe as our baby girl is placed in them.

Cass holds her tight, and gently strokes the cheek of our sleeping daughter. I reach over and feel the soft skin beneath my fingertips, and I'm struck speechless.

"And here's baby number two." I move back so the nurse can place our son on the other side of Cassidy's chest.

She's looking down at them as if she can't believe they're actually here, her eyes wide in wonder. As I take in the image in front of me, I feel my chest tighten inexplicably.

Six months ago I never would have believed I could be any happier than the moment Cassidy and I stood in front of an Elvis impersonator, and got married in the cheesiest Vegas chapel we could find. But I was wrong. Because here, *now*, I have never been happier, or as full of love as I am in this moment, with my family in front of me.

"They're beautiful, right? It's not just me being biased?" Cassidy's voice sounds stronger, and I smile at the pride in her voice.

"Fuck no, they're the most beautiful babies ever. But what did you expect, they're *our* babies."

"Fuck yeah, they are."

"We'll have to make some more pretty soon, I think." I say this unthinkingly as I stroke our son's head, feeling the silky softness of his fine hair, and when I look up Cassidy is shooting me daggers.

"You and your dick can stay the hell away from me until these two are at least five years old, Sunshine. Don't think that was an empty threat I made earlier." I laugh loudly at her bold declaration. I'll put money on her jumping me as soon as she's given the all clear. She likes my cock way too much. Needing to change the subject quickly when my dick starts to twitch at the idea of getting jumped by my wife, I turn to her and ask, "So, names? We're still happy with what we chose?"

"Yep, I love them. Those are my babies' names," she whispers with a soft smile.

Kissing the tops of both babies' heads, I close my eyes against the wave of emotion that strikes me.

"Welcome to our family, Mackenzie Rose," I trace my finger along her tiny upturned nose, "and Sebastian Jack."

THE END.

I hope you enjoyed *Dandelion Dreams*! Keep reading for a sneak peek at book 3 in the *Finding Forever* series, *Amongst the Wildflowers* (Layla's story!), and please consider leaving a review.

***

Would you like a FREE book? Get your copy of Rule Breaker, a steamy student/teacher rom com, HERE!

***

Also, don't miss the sneak peek of *Letting Him Go* by Eva Jones at the end of this book, which is AVAILABLE NOW!

SNEAK PEEK: Amongst the Wildflowers by Amali Rose

PROLOGUE

LAYLA

*M*y legs are on fire and my lungs about to burst, but I push myself forward, distancing myself from the words. *Those words.* The hate they throw at me, making me want to curl up and disappear.

Arms pumping, I burst into the field behind my home and immediately fall in a heap amongst the beauty of the wildflowers, shoulders shaking as I purge the bitterness rioting through my body.

Seconds pass unknowingly and with each beat of my heart, the sobs wrack my body. His approach goes unseen, but I hear the rustle of flowers as he takes his place on the hard ground next to me.

Wordlessly, his pinkie finger wraps around my own and a calmness envelops me. Oblivious to time, we lay there, and I allow his steady breath to soothe me, the way his presence always does.

What could be minutes, or hours later, he stands,

unfolding his lanky frame and reaches out for me. Without hesitation I take hold, his warm, strong grasp filling me with strength.

He's got me. He's always got me.

CHAPTER ONE

LAYLA

*M*y eyes wander around the library, taking in the quiet serenity that I love so much. There is nothing in this world that beats the atmosphere of a library. The sense of peace, the smell of books and the power of knowledge held within these walls. It all combines to create a heady sense of intoxication. Casting another glance around, this time I notice a small group of girls whispering and giggling as they play around on their phones, ignoring the work scattered around in front of them.

Okay, well, it's possible it's just me that feels so strongly about them.

Sighing, my hand unconsciously finds my glasses and pushes them up the bridge of my nose before I check my phone for the eighteenth time in the last thirty minutes. The paper I'm supposed to be writing sits pointlessly on the table in front of me while I wonder where Evie could be.

Realizing my next class begins in twenty minutes

and I need to get going, I close my textbooks and begin to pack away my things, worrying my bottom lip between my teeth the entire time. It's not like Evie to stand me up.

Just as I slide the last of my things into my backpack, Evie comes barreling through the aisles toward me, huffing and puffing and garnering plenty of dirty looks on her way.

As always, I'm struck by her easy dismissal of other people's opinions. She is oblivious to the hostility she's receiving, her focus on me never wavering. I, on the other hand, can feel my face flush as her entrance throws unwanted attention my way.

"I know, I know, I know! I'm sorry, but I have a good reason, I swear!"

My eyes trail down her body, taking in her frazzled appearance. Her brown hair is pulled up in a purposefully messy bun, but it has come loose at some point and a few long tendrils are stuck to her red, sweaty face. But what immediately grabs my attention is a large red stain spread across her white t-shirt that causes me to feel slightly faint.

"Is that blood?" I can't disguise the disgust in my voice and despite my lightheadedness growing worse at just the idea of a bloody wound on her abdomen, I begin planning our trip to the emergency room. What if I have to look at it? My eyes widen in horror at the thought and I plop my butt on the chair closest to me, sucking in air.

"What?" Her voice is curious as she looks down at herself and her fingers go straight to the stain, her face scrunching up in annoyance. Turning back to face me, she laughs loudly at my hunched-over-almost-hyper-ventilating form.

"Oh my God, relax, it's just ketchup." Evie gives me a look that is far too judgmental, in my opinion, as I process this information and feel my body return to normal.

"Lay, you do realize that you're going to be a grade school teacher, right? A teacher to tiny little germ-infested humans, who are pretty much constantly covered in some kind of bodily fluid?"

I hold my hand up to stop her, as my stomach starts to drop again, but she's on a roll.

"Blood, snot, spew... oh my God, poop! You'll totally have to deal with poop at some stage! How are you going to cope?"

"You know, you're not helping my situation right now." I roll my eyes at her dramatics. "I mean, yeah, I'm not great with blood but really? It's not like all of that will be a daily occurrence, right? I'm going to be a teacher, not a nurse."

"Whatever," she shrugs. "All I know is I used to babysit a six-year-old and he was always covered in something disgusting. Kids are kind of gross, Lay. You need to be prepared for that shit." She laughs loudly. "Metaphorically *and* literally!"

Taking hold of my hand, she drags me along, pulling me toward the exit. "C'mon, we need to haul ass or we're going to be late to art history."

I blink against the muted sunlight as we leave the library and head toward the arts building across the quad. Fallen leaves crunch under our feet and the crispness of the air reminds me autumn is here and leaves me craving a pumpkin-spiced latte. Those things are the bomb diggity and don't ever let anyone tell you otherwise.

I link my arm through Evie's as we stroll across campus, in a much more leisurely fashion than we should. Normally, I would be racing, but our art history professor, Professor Sims, is notorious for being late to class.

"So, why were you late and why do you have that God-awful stain on your shirt?"

"Oh! I was running late because Jessie caught me after Psych and wanted to borrow my notes from a class she missed. *Then* I needed to grab something from the food court, because I was starving, and this uber hottie crashed into me and smooshed his hot dog against me!" Leaning her head against mine, she waggles her eyebrows conspiratorially. "Unfortunately, I'm not speaking literally, 'cause dude was hot and I would be more than happy to acquaint myself with his hot dog, if you get my meaning."

I giggle at her lame innuendo. "Yeah, I don't think you're as subtle as you think you are."

"Aw, sugar plum, I can do graphic if that's what you prefer."

"I'm good, but thanks anyway," I answer wryly.

Evie straightens suddenly, nudging my shoulder. "Speaking of doable hot dogs, look who's over there."

I follow her gaze and spot Michael Bradshaw lounging on the grass with a group of fellow football players. My breath catches in my throat, and when I notice his head start to turn my way, I immediately avert my eyes and duck my head down.

My crush on Michael is ridiculous, I'm the first to admit this. He's the star quarterback, most popular guy on campus and if rumors are to be believed, he is also a total manwhore. Which is exactly why he's not for me, and I shouldn't be making gooey heart eyes at him across the quad.

But he's also the first guy to make my girly senses tingle since... well, let's not go there. Suffice to say, he's the unicorn I didn't think existed, which is why I don't beat myself up too much when my eyes seek him out anytime he's within a five-mile radius. There's no harm in dreaming, right?

"When are you going to talk to him, already? You two would make such a cute couple." Evie's voice interrupts my thoughts and I barely control the snort that wants to escape in response to that little gem.

"Yeah, the hot QB and the chubby, plain, nerdy girl. It's a match made in heaven, I'm sure."

"Okay, I'm going to ignore the chubby, plain remark, because you're stubborn as hell, and frankly I'm tired of telling you you're sexy AF. But the hot QB and the nerd *is* a match made in heaven. Hell, I can name at least ten books off the top of my head, that proves that point."

I use every ounce of my self-control to keep my eyes from rolling. "In *books* Evie, not real life. In real life, the hot QB dates the hot cheerleader." I pause as I consider this. "Or he sluts around with any hot chick that will spread her legs for him. And both are perfectly valid life choices. More power to them. But nowhere do I fit in that story, and that's okay. I'm perfectly content to ogle all that pretty from afar."

"Whatever, liar. We'll talk about this later."

Fortunately, we reach the arts building and Evie lets the subject drop as we make our way into the lecture hall. The class is filling up already and the noise of raucous voices and laughter echoes around us as we take our seats at the back of the auditorium, near the door. Art History is my last class of the day and considering it's Friday, I'm eager to make a quick exit when it's all done.

"Hey, you want to go out for a drink tonight? It's two dollar shot night at *Hound Dog*." She eyes me beseechingly as I consider her offer. I have an English paper I really need to work on, but I really could do with a night out. Between my work at *Books & Beans* and preparing for the school year, it's been way too long since I had a bit of fun.

"Why not?"

Evie grasps my hands, her face alight with excitement. "Oh, thank God! I thought I was going to have to start bribing you with donut holes to get you out of the dorm room, and my wallet really can't handle that kind of pressure."

"Jeez, exaggerate much? I haven't been that bad." My brow furrows. "Have I?"

"Lay, you've hardly left the dorm this week. I get that it's the first week of school and you want to 'start as you mean to go on,'" my eyes narrow at her use of air quotes. "But you need to find balance. All work and no play makes you…" Her voice trails off. "Well, boring. It makes you boring, Layla." Shrugging her shoulders, she quirks an eyebrow at me.

I sigh quietly at her observation. It's possible I might have been a bit too enthusiastic this week, but it's my final year at college and I just want it to go as smoothly as possible. It seemed like a good idea to throw myself into my studies, but even I have to admit that after only five days it's already getting old. "Okay, point taken. But if you think for one second, you're getting me drunk on cheap and nasty shots, you're mistaken."

"We'll see, I guess." I do my best to ignore the mischievous tone in her voice and all its implications.

Professor Sims chooses this moment to arrive, and we go about settling in for today's lesson while the professor's melodic voice starts going through the course syllabus.

While I am far from artistic myself, I'm a huge art lover and I have been so excited to take this course. My eyes are glued to the front of the class, keenly absorbing all the information we are being given, and my concentration is focused so completely it takes a few punches to my arm for Evie to get my attention.

"What!" I hiss as quietly as possible.

"It's him! The hottie!" She motions with her eyes to the door, and I swivel my neck to see who has her all excited.

The hairs on the back of my neck stand on end and

my heart rate doubles as I look at the guy standing there.

It couldn't be. Surely, I would have heard if he was back in town.

Unable to tear my deprived eyes away, I trail them up and down, noting and devouring everything about him. The always-mussed dark brown hair, so familiar, reminding me of the years we shared. The masculine scruff covering his jaw, so different, reminding me of the years that have passed.

His stance as he stands at the entrance to the auditorium, is confident, and his bright hazel eyes are alight with amused interest as he scans the room, however his expression changes to one that could almost be described as relief as his gaze clashes with mine. My stomach drops as he immediately heads in our direction.

Glancing at Evie, I notice she is practically bouncing in her seat as she follows his path toward us. Meanwhile, I'm trying to slouch down in my own seat in an attempt to make myself invisible, desperate to avoid what I know is coming. My cheeks flame as I see a pair of black Chucks stop in front of my seat, and I slowly raise my eyes to meet his.

"Hey, Bug."

Amongst the Wildflowers is **AVAILABLE NOW!**

Stay Connected

Private Facebook Group: https://www.facebook.com/
groups/amalisrisqueromantics
BookBub: https://www.bookbub.com/
authors/amali-rose
Facebook: https://www.
facebook.com/authoramalirose
Goodreads: https://www.goodreads.com/author/
show/17064277.Amali_Rose
Instagram: https://www.
instagram.com/authoramalirose
TikTok: https://vm.tiktok.com/ZS3KAon3/

My newsletter is the best way to stay in contact with
me! You'll get first look at titles, covers and release
dates, plus exclusive sneak peeks!
Sign up here: https://tinyurl.com/y6h3hw9s

More by Amali Rose

Finding Forever Series
(Standalone series)

Under the Cherry Blossoms >> Fling to Forever
Romance
Dandelion Dreams >> Enemies to Lovers/Office
Romance
Amongst the Wildflowers >> Friends to Lovers
Romance
Breathing Wisteria >> Second Chance Romance
Finding Forever>> The Complete Series

Greetings From Avondale Series
(Standalone Series)

Mistletoe Mistake >> Brother's Best Friend/Holiday
Romance
Miss Independent >> Billionaire Romance

Standalones:

Dating the DILF >> Single Dad Romantic Comedy

ACKNOWLEDGMENTS

Oh my god, guys, this book! It just about killed me! I have to say, Cassidy caught me by surprise. I fell in love with her when I was writing *Under the Cherry Blossoms*, and it seems that a lot of you agreed. I was inundated with people wanting her story, which I was so excited to do!

But then I sat down to write, and I struggled. Really struggled. I wanted Cassidy to surprise you, and make you fall in love with her soft side as much as you loved her brash side. I wanted to give her the story she deserved, and the man that she deserved. I hope that I did it. I truly love this story. I love Cassidy and Mason. Both separately and together, and I hope that you love it, and them, as much as I do.

My alpha readers: Kim, Tanya and Joz. You guys kept this story on track every step of the way. You motivated me when I didn't think I could do it, and you held me accountable, making sure I wrote the very best story I could. Thank you so much for that. I love you guys!!!!

A special thank you to Kim. You lived this story with me. You listened to me bitch and moan and stress, and you never once doubted this book would get finished. You are a freaking rock star!

My beta readers: Ashley, Brenda, Rachel, Tamara & Tre. Your feedback throughout this process was invaluable, and I can't thank you enough for dropping whatever you were doing anytime I sent you chapters to read. You girls are incredible, and I'm so grateful for everything.

My girl, Joz. You think you know how I feel about you. Times it by a million and you might be close. Thank you for being you.

The Sassy ladies! Joz, Kim, Harper, Laura, Sienna & Stacey. I don't know what I would do without you all, and I hope I never find out. I will have your back until the very end. Love you!!!

Tanya, you're one of the best people I know. I can't wait for the day I can squeeze you again! Love your guts!

Rachel. My favourite kiwi!!! Thank you for stepping up and helping me with the Street Team. I appreciate it more than you know. You are such a special person, and I'm so lucky to have you as a friend.

Kerry & Karen. I think we can all agree that 2017 kicked our asses a little bit! But I have a good feeling about 2018. New babies (C'mon Walter!) and new jobs, we're going to be kicking ass and taking names! I love you both so much. We got this.

Ben Ellis from Tall Story, you make magic! Thank you for such an amazing cover!

Stacey Broadbent & Petrina Jenkins from Spell Bound. You ladies put up with a lot of crap from me with this book! Thank you for understanding and being so flexible with me. You are such a pleasure to work with, and you do a wonderful job. I'm lucky to have found you, thank you!

Nikki and Lauren from Saints and Sinners Book Promotions. You ladies are fabulous to work with, and I can't thank you enough for everything you do for me, helping to spread the word about my books. I hope we get the chance to work together many more times!

My ST, Amali's Sinful Sweethearts: Antonette, Cassy, Devon, Heather, Katrina, Kristi, Lauren, Rachel, Tamara & Tre. Thank you all for your unwavering support and encouragement. Please don't ever underestimate how much I appreciate everything you do for me!

Finally, to the wonderful bloggers who bust their asses promoting indie authors. You have my eternal gratitude. The job you do demands your time, your passion and your dedication. I am in complete awe of you all!

Huge love and hugs!
Amali xox

ABOUT THE AUTHOR

USA Today Bestselling author Amali Rose is a former blogger from Australia, who released her debut novella in 2017.

A self confessed bookworm, her love affair with the written word began as a child, with *The Magic Faraway Tree*. Her tastes have grown and evolved over the years and, after stumbling into the indie community a few years ago, she discovered her passion for romance with a side of smut.

When not reading or writing, Amali enjoys cheesy pop music, netflix marathons, and she believes strongly that pink, puppies and chocolate make the world a better place!

SNEAK PEEK: Letting Him Go by Eva Jones

"Hey Mom, I'm heading to the mall with Amy," I call through the bathroom door, not waiting for a response before my feet hit the carpeted steps and I'm out the front door, hopping into my best friend Amy's waiting car. Summer breaks back at home had always been my favorite. It's bittersweet that I've graduated and there'll be no heading back to the apartment that Amy and I've shared for the past four years. Time to enter the real world.

"Girl, what took you so long? I feel like I've been sitting out here for hours." Her voice raises an octave as if she seriously had been waiting years and not just the five minutes. "Let me guess… Travis."

My cheeks hurt as I smile. "Yeah, I've missed him. That was the longest time we've ever gone not seeing each other."

"Geez girl. Can you rein in the cheesy smile for just a minute?" Laughing, her arm swings and smacks my shoulder before she shifts the car in drive and peels out of my driveway. "Let the girl's day begin!"

We spend half the day getting mani-pedis and gossiping about the newest couple at school and finding the perfect outfits for Troy Michel's party tonight. I have the biggest news ever to tell Travis, and even though we love each other to the moon and back and we're going to spend the rest of our lives together, I don't know how he's going to take it. My stomach is completely knotted up as I slip into the soft peach satin dress that I picked out at the mall. Amy said that it's perfect on me, but the spaghetti straps and extremely low-cut neckline are giving me second thoughts. It's not that I'm a prude, I just don't feel comfortable putting all my goods out there. Like what if a tit pops out? The embarrassment would just kill me. But for Travis, I'll take that chance tonight. Besides, Amy talked me into buying some boob tape today, she worships it, this stuff better be the best invention since Pop-Tarts. I'm just going to keep my fingers crossed and hope it's all she talked it up to be.

The sound of the doorbell ringing echoes through the house right before I hear Travis yells up the stairs. "Hey babe, it's just me. You about ready to go?"

"Yeah just give me one more sec and I'll be right down."

I turn back to the mirror which stretches down the whole length of my bedroom door. My hands glide smoothly over the satin of my dress as I try to ensure the boob tape is doing its job. I twirl a few of my tousled light brown loose curls around my fingers and put them back in their place. Slipping my feet into my nude stiletto heels, I make my way down the steps, holding the railing to keep my balance.

"Okay, I'm ready, hon."

Travis is standing at the breakfast bar, his head tilted down toward his phone. He turns to me and the moment his crystal blue eyes hit me, tingles shoot down my spine. It barely takes him two strides before he's in front of me, the sweet caress of his lips doing nothing to help my brain function in that moment.

"Trav, we gotta get going."

"Can't we just call it a night and stay in?" He whispers the last part into my ear, my body heating to the core. I take a step back to try to regain some control over myself, knowing my mom should be getting home from her second shift job at any moment and no matter how old I am, this is most certainly not something I want her walking into.

"Travis, we gotta go. I told Amy we'd pick her up so that she didn't have to arrive alone."

"Fine, okay. But only because I know what a good friend you are, and I know you don't want to flake on her." He pulls me in, and his mouth connects with mine, he shows me all his wants and needs in one single kiss.

It's quiet on the car ride over to Amy's and I can't help but be nervous. What if he's not ready? Shit, I'm not even ready. A little too late now, right?

"Babe, you okay over there? You look a million

miles away right now." His hand reaches over and engulfs mine as he entwines our fingers.

"I'm not really sure to be honest, Trav." He immediately pulls over to the side of the road and throws the car in park. I wasn't expecting to have this conversation now, but I've never held back or lied to him before. Why start now?

"Tell me what's going on, Ken. I'm here for you, no matter what. You know that, right?"

"Yes, I know. But this is kind of a biggie. It's not really something you should just throw out there."

"Just tell me wha—"

"I'm pregnant." I didn't mean to blurt it out, but it just came out. Like an oversized balloon ready to burst.

Little did I know, ten months later, one fatal accident would change life as I knew it.

CHAPTER ONE

KENNY

Ten Years Later

"Does the victim advocate have anything she'd like to add?" Judge Miller asks.

"Yes, Judge. Kennedy Stewart, from the Claymore House for battered women, representing Monica Young."

"And what do you have to say on the case?" The judge speaks directly to me as I approach the bench with Monica at my side.

"The defendant entered Ms. Young's home uninvited on the night in question, where he took it upon himself to steal valuables. When she woke, he decided it was a good time to physically assault her, sending her to the emergency room with a concussion and stitches on her cheekbone." I signal to the file in front of him.

"The prosecutor already supplied the photos. I'm here to get restitution for the doctor and emergency room bills. In addition to that, either the property which was taken or restitution to be paid directly to her for replacement of said taken items."

I can't help but look over at the man with a scowl on my face. No matter how many years I've been doing this job, or how closed off I keep my heart, these cases still get to me. It's possible that's why I do so well at the job at hand, but good Lord why do people treat others whom they claim to love this way? I'll just never understand it, and I hope the judge gives Bradley, AKA scumbag, the full nine months on the table.

"Would the victim like to say a word?" the judge asks, and Monica moves slightly behind me. Her arm is linked through mine and I feel her start to shake. I reach up with my other hand and give her a reassuring squeeze.

"No, Your Honor, she would prefer not to speak at this time for fear of backlash if she does. On that note, we'd like to ask for a civil restraining order to go into effect once the defendant is released."

"And so, it's ordered. A restraining order goes into effect at the time of release. As for the charges, the maximum sentence allowed is up to nine months in prison. The defendant has entered a guilty plea; therefore, I will commence sentencing now." The judge is hastily writing and signing papers as he speaks. "In the case of Young versus Santiago, full restitution is to be made to the plaintiff and a sentence of the full nine months, to start on the day first incarcerated, with a possibility of parole after six months. There is to be no contact with Ms. Young upon release. If the order is broken, it will be a violation of your parole and you will be subject to the time left on your sentence and any charges that ensue. You are dismissed." The sound of the gavel echoing in the courtroom propels everyone toward the exit.

"Thank you, Judge Miller," I give one final thanks as I always do before turning to walk away, but the judge's voice stops me mid-turn.

"No, thank you, Kennedy. For all that you do. You may not think it's a lot, but you help give these women the voice they have a hard time finding in these situations."

I give him a nod and a tight smile, pick up my file and turn to escort Monica to the exit. She thanks me and leaves out through the back entrance. It's my last case of the day, and with the frustration and relief from today's cases still hanging over me, I head toward the makeshift office I use and gather my things to leave.

On top of everything else, today is the birthday of my daughter's dad and every year I pick her up from school early, we head to the grocery store to buy a cake, and then spend a couple of hours at the cemetery with him. This year will be no different. Despite our hardships, Grace has grown into a wonderful girl; he would have been so proud. She's outgoing, smart, funny, and always looks on the bright side of things. She's my light when I think everything has gone dark. She's what keeps me moving when I've lost all strength. One look into her emerald green eyes, the very same as his, and I know that I must push on and give her my all.

I pull into the school turnaround and head in to sign Grace out. She's already sitting there waiting for me with a big smile on her face.

"Hey honey, you ready?" I pull her into a tight hug which she returns with equal fervor. I've never been one for public displays of affection, but with her, all cards are off the table.

"Yep I'm ready, even made Dad a birthday card in art class today."

I pull her close as the sadness in her voice causes my heart to contract. We fall into an uneasy silence before she suddenly perks up and a huge smile lights up her beautiful face.

"Oh my gosh Mom, you won't believe who said hi to me today."

Attempting to hide a smile, I have a feeling I know who she's going to say. She's had the biggest crush on our next -door neighbor's son for as long as I can remember, but he's a year older and never really gave her the time of day after he started school.

"Hmm let me think… could it have been Cameron?" I laugh, my arm around her shoulders as we walk back to my car.

"Yes Mom!" she practically yells it to me. "Can you believe it? He hasn't even spoken to me since like, the fifth grade. I didn't even know he still remembered who I even was anymore." She's literally jumping up and down as she gets into the car.

"Well Grace you have known each other almost your entire lives, how could he ever forget who you are?"

"Yeah, I guess you're right. But I'm still super excited that he talked to me," she says while buckling her seat belt. "Are we heading to the store for the cake?" Her voice is curious as I pull out of the school turnaround.

"Yeah. Did you decide what type of cake you want to get this time?" I always let her choose.

"Can we get marble with buttercream frosting? I didn't like whatever kind of frosting they used on the last cake we bought for your birthday."

"Yes, baby we can."

We get our cake and a bouquet of flowers and make our way to the cemetery. The trip doesn't take long because we only live one town over from his resting place, I wanted to make sure that she could visit whenever she wanted. I also spend a lot of time there just talking to him when life gets too much.

We lay out a blanket and set up the cake. I pull a pack of candles from my purse, put them on the cake and light them, placing the cake in front of her.

We sing happy birthday to Travis while snuggled up together in the blanket.

"Make a wish and blow out the candles for him, honey."

Her eyes are closed like she is concentrating very hard, then she bends and blows them all out in one try.

"What did you wish for honey?" I can't help but be curious.

"I can't tell you Mom, or it won't come true," she responds with a sad look on her face.

"Okay Grace, but you know if you ever need to talk about anything, I'm here for you." I pull her in for a hug.

"I know Mom. The thing is... my wish was for you."

"What do you mean, honey? What could you possibly wish for me? I have everything I want and need right here."

My arms wrap tighter around her, but she pulls back with her head down, twisting grass between her fingers like she's nervous.

"Mom, you haven't dated since Dad. You've not even tried, and I know men ask. Susie Parks told me about her dad asking you to dinner, and you said no." She pauses briefly. "And for an old guy, he's actually kind of cute." She giggles, but it's sad, and I feel my eyes glisten at the sound. "I want you to find love like we see in all those chick flicks we watch on movie night."

I watch helplessly as tears start to fill her eyes.

"Grace, I swear to you, I'm happy. I'm happy with it being you and me."

"But Mom, don't you want your happily ever after?" Her voice falls away as she struggles to find the words. "I know you loved Dad with all of your heart, but that doesn't mean you can't find love again. It won't hurt me if you do, Mom, I'd understand."

"Baby, I'm okay. I promise." I pull her close and kiss the top of her head, willing the tears not to fall in front of her.

Letting Him Go by Eva Jones is AVAILABLE NOW!

.

www.ingramcontent.com/pod-product-compliance
Lightning Source LLC
Chambersburg PA
CBHW030421120726
47903CB00003B/757